Antho

A collection 　　　　 　　 　it
stories, tall tales, 　　　 .rageous
taradid.es

Sarah Hitchcock

First published in England 2020

ISBN 978-1-8382034-0-5

For Mum

Because she even likes the toffees

Contents

Introduction

An anthology of short stories is such a bag of Revels it barely needs mentioning – you never know what you are going to get next, especially, I will admit freely, within this particular selection of tales. I'm sorry to start with such an overused cliché but sometimes the old ones are the best ones. These stories have no theme running through to link them, no thread to tie them nicely together, no over-arching motif. The only link is that they all came out of my head. I offer you a mish-mash of toffees, orange creams and maltesers, with the occasional surprising coconut, and always welcome chocolate button.

Some of these stories have been written for events or competitions, some just for my own pleasure and some to stop the brain-itch of holding too many words inside. I haven't arranged them in chronological order or indeed, you may think after reading a few, in any logical order at all. Just to throw you of balance and to refer back to the slightly queasy horror of eating Revels, I have put dark tales next to silly ones, happy next to sad, science fiction next to fairy tale next to fable. There are no romances, turn back now if that's what you are after – you don't get strawberry creams in a bag of Revels.

The good thing about a collection of short stories is that you don't have to start at the beginning. Pick a title and start where you like – read the long ones first to get them out of the way – the short ones on the loo – the ones that make you laugh in a crowded train (this was written before social distancing rules applied). Use the book as you would that pesky bag of chocolates – gorge yourself sick, or savour each piece of confectionary to make the most of its unique and peculiar quality and make the bag last. However you chose to devour these stories, I hope you have fun doing so. They are totally guilt free and in no way will they make you fat – unless, of course, they inspire you to lie on the sofa all day reading books and eating Revels.

So, don't expect a luxury box of Belgian chocolates within these pages but an everyday bag of sweets, hopefully with something for everyone.

The Day I Took My Zombie to Alton Towers

A few years ago, I moved into an old Victorian house on the outskirts of Swindon. It has one of those attics that you access via a proper staircase, and floorboards, and a tiny round window. It was probably the maid's room. In the corner, sitting on a rickety chair and covered in a thick layer of dust, was a zombie.

We hit it off immediately.

I quickly realised she couldn't speak – you need a functioning tongue to be able to form words and breath to make sound come out. She can just about manage a low moaning. I spent the best part of a week trying out different names to find one she would respond to, and now she's called Susan. She has a particular way of moaning: sort of 'hmmmmrrraaaaah', which I think is her trying to say my name … Janice.

Susan is very dry for a zombie, not that I've had much experience with the un-dead, but there's nothing rotting or bad smelling about her, otherwise I wouldn't let her in the kitchen. She's just very desiccated and papery, and has a musty odour like old books. I used to be a librarian so I'm used to the smell and actually find it rather pleasant. Because of her dryness she's quite brittle and, as a consequence, extremely fragile. I mist her every day with a plant atomiser filled with spring water and a touch of lavender oil. It seems to help but we do still have the odd accident. Once, due to an ill-advised choice of footwear –

flip-flops no less – she lost a little toe when it got caught in a drain cover. It disappeared into the sewer system below with a sad 'plink'. I would have stuck it back if we could have retrieved it: I'm a great believer in UHU.

Footwear and clothes in general are something of a problem – I won't let her go about naked as she would prefer, I do have standards. Everything she wears has to completely undo: the idea of pulling anything on or off is unthinkable due to the high risk of limb loss. I made the mistake of putting a pair of marigolds on her once so she could help about the house and it took us the whole day and a box set of Downton Abbey to ease them off without any damage. As it was, she lost a couple of nails and a thumb pad got stuck irreversibly to the rubber, but otherwise the gloves are still perfectly usable.

Susan likes to read and watch things on the U-tube. She has very opaque, milky eyes so it's a wonder she can see at all. I had to get her three pairs of the strongest over-the-counter reading glasses, which she wears one on top of the other. We've also strapped two high-powered magnifying glasses together. I think she can only see a few letters at a time so reading anything other than a menu takes a lot of perseverance on her part. I think it shows great strength of character. Of course, I have to make sure she stays out of direct sunlight when she's using the lenses due to the risk of incineration. Even with the misting, as I've said, she's very dry. Once, due to an unfortunate spark from the open fire, her legs caught alight. I doused her immediately with the vase of chrysanthemums that was at hand but we've never been able to get the scorch marks out. Not even leather upholstery cleaner seems to work on dehydrated flesh.

As I've said, Susan has a strong character and that is to be applauded. However, recently our normally tranquil home life has been disturbed. We've been at odds with one another! I take Susan out; it's not as if I don't. We go to the local library for Mills and Boon and take walks in the park – well I walk and she lurches, more so since her legs crisped up in the fire – so I was a little upset when she started leaving adverts for family attractions in places she knew I would find them: pasted to the back of the Kellogg's bran flakes box, stuck under the loo seat, and slipped between the pages of Reader's Digest. The latest mania is for Alton Towers. I told her in no uncertain terms that a trip to an amusement park for someone of her condition would be more than ill-advised, it would be madness.

We're going next Tuesday.

What can I say, she wore me down with a relentless and, I have to admit, well thought through campaign. She would do well in local government. It wasn't just the endless leaflets, or the posters stuck to every surface that got to me, it was the moaning, literally, the moaning. All night she would pace the landing carrying a placard that read: 'Cruelty to the Un-dead', whilst loudly moaning. I was afraid the neighbours would hear. The last straw was when she wrote me a note warning that if I didn't take her to Alton Towers, she would report me to Childline. I wasn't too worried about her ringing a phone service due to her speech difficulty but I do worry that they might have a website … she's become very adept at surfing the net and she can be eloquently persuasive in prose. I don't want the authorities round here, I'm not sure they would accept my explanations for the missing toe and blackened knees.

Alton Towers is vast, crowded and, to my mind, a little trashy but Susan loves it. I have insisted she goes in the wheelchair and wears a large wide-brimmed hat and sunglasses. It saves people staring and asking what's wrong with her. I manage to keep her away from the big dippers by taking her to Cbeebies land and giving her several goes on the Postman Pat ride, but after lunch I take a wrong turn and we find ourselves right in front of something called Oblivion.

There's no dissuading Susan.

The ride boasts of being one of the highest G-force roller coasters in the UK.

Nothing good can come of this.

Susan's hat blows off first taking an ear with it, quickly followed by her sunglasses. We've been given strict instructions to keep our hands in the car so, naturally, Susan waves at someone on the ground just as we start the big drop. The level of screaming behind us takes on a new timbre as Susan's hand lands in a lady's lap.

As we disembark and I'm shoving Susan's stump into the pocket of her pinafore, we're greeted by a very worried looking official. I hastily retrieve the hand from the still screaming woman and begin to explain:

'It was a prank – in poor taste, I agree, look, it's only rubber,' I wave it at the official who goes from worried to irate.

'Susan has a condition,' I explain quickly, settling her back into her wheelchair.

This makes everyone suddenly uncomfortable: you can't shout at a person with a 'condition'.

'Well, no harm done,' says the official. 'Bless her, look at that expression, she really enjoyed that ride!'

It's only then that I catch a glimpse of Susan's face.

Oh, dear God!

The speed of the ride has nearly blown her face off! Her eyes are goggling wide and her lips have been blasted away from her teeth into a rictus grin of immense proportions.

I jam my own sunglasses onto her, to hold her eyeballs in place and we hurry away. Behind us I hear someone say: 'Poor love, did you see, she only had one ear.'

If she wasn't already dead, I'd kill Susan for this.

Back in the car I try and re-arrange her features to look more normal but I'm unable to wipe the grin off her face. We don't speak all the way down the M6. Well, I don't and Susan wisely keeps her moaning to herself.

'Never again,' I say as we get to the first roundabout in Swindon. 'It's the park or the library or nothing from now on.'

Susan rustles in her handbag and pulls out a sheet of paper. I have to swerve into the bus lane as she holds it in front of my face. It's an online booking confirmation for a bungee jump off Bristol suspension bridge.

I stare at her, for the first time, in genuine horror.

One of Susan's now baggy eyelids slides shut in a wink.

A Very Small Old Lady

I was in Wilkinsons the other day and something shuffled past: it was a very small old lady. She was wearing a green overcoat and a brown felt hat, was very neat and smart, and was just adorable; I wanted to keep her. She was at the till when I finished shopping, rummaging for coins in an oversized purse. Her cashier was the big soft lad with the curly red hair. He was leaning over his counter smiling indulgently at her. I could see he wanted to keep her too.

She finished paying and left, getting a bit confused with the automatic doors, which was just the cutest thing. The cashier then noticed one of her small brown gloves on the floor by his till. He raced after her into the echoing shopping precinct, waving the tiny article over his head. We were all a bit stunned: it only left one cashier! I had to wait quite some time as the customer in front of me had several items that weren't priced properly. There was an argument and the manager came over. He sorted it by having a bit of a shout too: it was all very Eastenders. When I left, the soft lad still wasn't back.

Thinking no more about him, I headed for the lifts and my car, boots tapping on the marble floor. I passed the budget clothes store and the lump of machinery that was supposed to make us appreciate the town's industrial heritage when, from round the corner where the pay machines for the multi-story are located, there came the most tremendous noise: the loudest burp I've ever heard. People coming out of the clothes store looked at me and started sniggering.

'It wasn't me,' I protested, and pointed in the direction of the burp, just as the very small old lady tripped round the corner.

The people from the shop laughed out loud and my face went red. They obviously thought I was shifting the blame; after all, such a sweet and tiny old thing couldn't possible have made such a noise. As she approached, I saw her lick her lips and pick something out of her teeth: it was a clump of orange hair. She slipped her brown gloves on and winked at me as she passed.

When I got to the pay machine I found a pair of size eleven shoes and a jumbled Wilko's uniform. There was no sign of the soft ginger lad.

The local Snooze and Journal reported that: according to popular opinion the red-headed cashier had finally lost the plot and was now running naked and free somewhere on the Cotswold Hills. The general public should exercise caution when approaching him. I knew better: it is very small old ladies who are the real danger, especially when they entice you away from the crowd with the old dropped-glove routine.

Siren Song

I wake in the deep night the sea thrumming in my ears, as silver light plays across the curtains. It briefly finds a way in through a gap to paint a line on the ceiling. I blink, muddled: the lighthouse at Start Point can't be seen from here. The light slides away before I'm fully awake, before I can tumble out of bed and across to the window. Head still thick and stupid with sleep, I pad the black-dark room, open the curtains wide, and catch my breath at a scene of wonder. Patches of stars are blurred, hazy and soft, as veils of cloud move unseen across the heavens. A glittering mass sharpens, bright and clear, uncovered, before fading to disappear as another cluster is revealed. On the horizon are winking lights smudged by distance and sea spray: fishing boats and cargo tankers ply the line between sky and sea; some barely a glowing dot, others a long blaze of consumerism lit bright.

Moonrise is not for a while so all else is dark. There's no sign of the light that woke me. Below the house the sea crashes against rocks, and from over the dark water comes the mournful song of seals. I'm drawn away from the warm soft chaos of bed, into jeans, and out the door to the black night. I don't need to see to navigate the path down to the cove: I've trod it too many times to count. The twisting descent is deep cut with use and arched-over in places with stunted trees and bushes sculpted into angles by salt-heavy winds. Here and there, in the late season's tired grass, pin-pricks of light glow green: the fire flies final chance of a mate before the days shorten and cold creeps back.

Down through the last section of path the darkness is complete. I can sense rather than see the mass of rock and earth towering up on my left and the sucking open space of the bay to my right. Sliding my feet forward in the blind night, I find the edge of the low wall that drops away to the beach and leave my shoes by the rusty hulk of an old winch. The ships are still sailing the horizon, bright in the night, but there's been no repeat of the silver beam that woke me. Maybe it was a fishing boat crossing the cove or maybe something from a dream. As my feet make contact with wet sand, I breathe deep and long, feeling the familiar thrill of kinship with the living entity that drew me here, away from bed and dreams: the sea.

In the east the sky has cleared leaving a few ragged remnants edged with soft light: the moon is coming. I walk out to the slapping sea. The tide has turned. Scalloped lines have been left on the shore, edged with tiny pebbles and broken shells – little gifts left behind by the running, rolling froth of waves as they retreat down the beach. I dig my toes into the gritty sand along one of these tide lines. An amoeba finger of spume stretches to envelope my feet with a cool caress before being sucked back into the sea. It leaves an offering balanced across my toes – a plastic spoon.

It feels like a reproach.

In my hands, the spoon is too smooth and has an alien warmth about it. Where has it come from? Was it amongst some rubbish dropped carelessly from a ship? Was it discarded on a beach along the coast after shovelling ice-cream into a sunburnt face? Was it thrown from a car to be washed along gutters, into drains, and down a river to the sea? This tiny weightless spoon settles on my heart like an iron bar: it bears the load of all pollution, everywhere. It's not just the floating debris that strangles and chokes, now it starves: breaking down to micro particles eaten by the bottom of the food chain, and concentrated all the way up, even to us. Still we won't learn, we don't stop, we make more. On the horizon the long lights of cargo ships head for port with more of the stuff, dozens of them coming night after night after night.

Across the tumbling sea comes the siren call of seals.

I strip, fold my clothes, and leave the spoon on top.

The sea pushes me about and I bob in its ever-moving embrace, relax into its rhythm, succumb to the shove and tug of this immense mass of water. I can believe the planet's alive when I'm drifting in the shifting sea – a precious fragile thing – our blue planet. I lay back and let myself float in the undulating darkness. It's so rare to experience true darkness but for a time I'm held, sightless in the vast, black, rocking sea – my physical self dissolved, my smallness eradicated for a moment as I touch the infinite.

The sound of surf breaking on the beach fades.

A whiskery touch snaps me back to myself and the here and now. Fear scatters my thoughts and my body stiffens – I go under, mouth filling with salt tang, thrashing, surfacing and gasping for air at the shock of it. I still can't see and now I'm afraid.

I'm not alone.

I tread water in a circle, heart racing. A quiet noise sends me spinning round – no more than a huff of breath, and the sound of water sliding. The moon, huge and white, lifts above clouds in the east. Silver light shivers over the water revealing a face close to mine – a strangely human face, light dancing in big soulful eyes – the seal, slick and lithe slips below the waves. A seal. What did I think it was going to be? My heart slows but only a little: I'm charged with the exhilaration of the encounter.

The moon rises and I can see the shore. With a twist of concern, I realise I've let the tide take me out with it. My body is numb from cold, my limbs heavy; it will take all my strength to get back.

I don't swim, not yet, I keep treading water, mesmerised at the way it slips and glitters as I move my pale arms beneath the surface. What am I waiting for? The moon finally breaks free of cloud. I'm bathed in silver, coated in it, and with this clean light comes clarity and a deep calm. On the shore I fancy I can see a faint spec where I left the spoon – a pale dot against the dark bulk of land – a cancerous cell. Behind me comes the soft sad call of the seal, the song flowing in time with the water's movement.

I turn and begin to swim.

New Glasses

'Ta Da!'

'Oh my God! Maisy—'

'Maz.'

'Maisy, what've you done?'

I shake my head to feel the short curls bounce around my ears, trying to recapture the elation I felt walking home.

'Had my hair cut,' I say. Inside I'm fighting the urge to punch her.

'All those beautiful golden curls – your crowning glory – how could you?'

'It was ginger frizz, mum.'

'And what are those? I preferred your old glasses; those make you look—'

'Trendy. I'm starting my new job Monday and want to look …'

'*Trendy!*'

Mum snorts and turns on the telly. I stare at the back of her head. Why does she always do this?

'Make us a cuppa, love; my favourite show's starting.'

Make your own you lazy cow – 'Yes, mum.'

On the way to the kitchen I look in the hall mirror. I look bloody brilliant and somehow that makes me really angry. I want to stamp about slamming doors – bugger her tea! But that would be childish and anyway *I* want a cuppa.

There's a burst of applause from the telly: *'on today's show we'll be meeting Charlene whose fiancé slept with all six bridesmaids on the night before their wedding. He's now the father of twins by the maid of honour and he expects them all to live as one big happy family.'*

God, why does she watch that crap? And she hasn't bothered to get dressed; she just slobs around in that bloody onesie watching shit daytime telly. I can't wait to get out. This job with the insurance firm is my ticket to freedom; my chance to really be me – a new me – the me I want to be – different and exciting me! Stumping back to the lounge, I slop tea on the hall carpet. So what? I don't care – it's a shit carpet – I'll mop it up in a minute. I push open the lounge door and drop the tea.

'Maisy—'

'Maz.'

'You clumsy idiot, get a cloth.'

I can't move – I'm transfixed. Mum pushes past, grumbling all the way to the kitchen. I can't tear my eyes from the telly: can't believe what I'm seeing. Mum pushes me out of the way again and dumps a pile of tea towels on the floor. She stamps on them to soak up the tea. I sit on the coffee table and lean forward to stare at the show's presenter.

'What the hell? Is this the Halloween special? Why's he got tusks?'

Mum slumps on the sofa, leaving the tea towels in a soggy brown heap. She pokes me in the back with her toe to get me to shift.

'What're you on about? He's no different to normal... maybe a bit more orange, and he's had his teeth whitened—'

'Are you kidding me? He's bloody green!'

'Language Maisy—'

'Maz – Look at him – he's green with tusks and hairy warts! He's a flippin' Ogre.'

'Oh for pity's sake, give it a rest! I know you don't like this show but there's no need to spoil it for *me*. He does a great service: really helps people.'

I look at her in disbelief but can see she believes what she's said. Back on the screen the audience is screaming and the couple have started fighting. They're being pulled apart by huge men in black tee shirts – except they're not men! Trolls! Bloody trolls and ogres! The host grins and gulps, his fat neck shudders and balloons.

'He's feeding off their emotions! Can't you see?'

'Stop it! Just stop it! You always spoil it. Go away! Go on, get out! Miss High-and-bloody-mighty-I'm-better-than-everyone-else, take your new glasses and your bloody *trendy* hair and go lecture some other poor sod.'

I feel the sting of tears so pull my glasses off to rub my eyes before she can see. I point at the telly as I fumble them back on, about to argue – Oh! The host and bouncers look normal. My stomach lurches; heat whooshes up my chest into my face – I'm going to throw up.

Been on my bed since I chugged up. It's dark but I haven't turned on the light. I'm trying to convince myself I'm not going mad: if it's not me, its mum; which makes more sense. After groping for my new glasses, I stumble to the window. There's still a little light in the sky and the houses opposite are black against deep violet. The street lamp makes the pavement orange; a moth stutters and stoops in the artificial glow. It's a big moth … really big! Christ Almighty, it's a bloody fairy!

I bang my head trying to get a better view and knock my glasses off. By the time I fumble them back on, the moth – or fairy – has gone. It's me then who's crazy. Bile burns my throat: don't *think* I'm mad – maybe it's my eyes? That's it! I pull my new glasses off and squint at them. Come to think of it, the lady who served me was pretty strange. The first thing she said was: *"Don't get many of your type in here."* I thought she was calling me a lesbian because of my new short hair but maybe she meant something else? And how come I was able to walk out with new glasses? It usually takes weeks. I look at the glasses – I do like them! I put them on and see my dim reflection in the dressing table mirror. Wow, I look good! What was it I was just worrying about?

'Maisy—'

'Maz,' I say under my breath.

There's a tentative knock and the door opens before I can say come in or go away. Mum snaps on the light and puts a mug of tea on the bedside table.

'There you go, love, you've been up here ages. I've brought you some Custard Creams too. Oh, and I found this photo; it's me and your Aunty Sharon, thought it might make you laugh. That's Margate seafront a week before you were born; was s'posed to be there with your father but he ran off the Wednesday before; went with Sharon instead seeing as I'd already paid for the B & B. Anyway, thought it would cheer you up.'

Mum slips the photo under the biscuits; it's her way of making everything alright again between us. Half way down the stairs she calls back:

'I'm doing Hawaiian pizza and garlic bread for tea – that ok?'

'Lovely,' I call back.

She won't put the pizza in; I'll have to do it. Picking up the photo, I brush off the crumbs. Mum and her sister look so young. They're wearing flowery dresses and mum's belly is enormous. They're grinning but it looks forced. My eyes fill up. I scrunch them shut. When I look again my heart stops: there's a man with his arms round mum, one hand on her belly; on me. It has to be dad: he's just the way mum always describes him; a young David Essex, with a gold hoop ear-ring and... pointed ears? That can't

24

be right! The Polaroid slips out of my fingers and spins away. I take my glasses off and jam my fists into my eyes. When my insides stop doing weird things I crawl under the bed to get the photo.

He'll be gone when I look again, of course he will: he wasn't there in the first place; none of the things have been there. I'm just anxious because of the new job. I look at the photo. Shit! He's still there, and now he's winking. I chuck the photo across the room followed by my new glasses. The damn things smash into the wall but aren't even scratched by the impact. Got to get rid of them. Stamping on them hurts my foot. Shit, will have to hide them then. In the wardrobe is a box bought to conceal love letters that I never got. I put the picture in with the glasses, lock it and jam it behind the dressing table, then drop the key through a gap in the floorboards. It's where I shove things I need to forget about. There's a diamond ring down there I pinched from Gran's jewellery box and a school report that said I had great potential and should be thinking of university. Done. I can breathe again. I find my old glasses and stare at my reflection; won't take long to grow my hair out too.

'Maisy, our favourite programme's starting; if you don't hurry you'll miss the first murder. Maisy?'

'Yes, mum, I'm coming.'

Under the floorboards, in a thick layer of dust and cobwebs, there's a diamond ring and a shredded report card; behind the dressing table, there's an empty box. Downstairs the telly blares and the smell of garlic pervades the house; outside fairies dance unobserved.

Rapunzel

She lets the silken tress slide through her fingers and fall, heavy to the floor. Stray golden threads catch on her chewed fingers and broken nails. She smoothes the shining waterfall, stretching her neck to ease the weight and shift the load. With a deep sigh, she runs the rake of a comb through the bountiful crop then begins to plait. At intervals she heaves the mass of coils into a slithering mound and flexes her neck and shoulders against the treasure's drag.

Outside, summer swifts scream across blue, slicing the sky with their flight.

Rapunzel finishes the plait.

She fixes it with thick nails, black iron, to the floor; hammering them deep, one, two, more and more, hammering herself to the floor. Then she pushes the great mass of gold, of her, out of the window. It falls with a sigh, tugging and snagging on the nails, swinging to stillness.

The high summer blue darkens to indigo.

Rapunzel waits, nailed to the floor.

Outside, an owl screeches across the dark, slicing the sky with its flight.

Clouds

'It's an elephant with no trunk ... or a bus.' I feel a giggle welling up and turn to Beth where she lies beside me staring up at the June sky.

'A hippo,' she murmurs without taking her eyes off the clouds.

'Yeah, a hippo,' I laugh. She always nails it. It's our favourite game in our favourite place: a shallow dip on the common out back of and above our home. It's nothing more than a dent in the earth but it cups us just right and all we can see lying down is a circle of grass and flowers, and the sky; the ever moving, changing sky. June is the best time here – the only time – when the grass is as tall as our knees, ram-rod straight, topped with a brush of purple or green-white. It ripples in waves, a susurrating ocean; tickling our out-stretched hands; whipping our bare legs. Buttercups – gold and shining; do-you-like-butter glowing under chins, staining white socks yellow – nod among the swishing stems.

She is smiling but her lips quiver and her face tightens. A star winks in the corner of her eye, swells and flashes, tumbling into her fanned out, corn-bright hair.

'I've missed you,' I whisper.

'I miss you,' she says.

I reach out to touch her cheek, thistledown on the wind. She catches the floating seed as it sweeps up and away, grasping it in her fist, crushing it fiercely she breathes a wish into her hand, eyes closed, wishing furiously, wishing and willing the wish to come true.

What are you wishing Beth?

She releases the fairy seed but her hot hand, tight fist of a hand has crumpled and dampened the tender spore. It won't fly, it won't come true.

'What did you wish, Beth?'

'I wish you were here.'

'I *am* right here.'

'I wish you weren't dead…'

She sobs quietly and I hold her in the sun's warmth, stroke her pale hair from her face with the tender breeze, kiss her cheek with a bee's wing. She smiles then, through the tears, and I know she can feel me. For a moment we are one; girls naming the shapes in the clouds, always here together, never here together again. Beth sits up and a veil begins to drop, shrouding her, me.

'I'll miss you,' I say.

'I miss you,' she says and pulls a crumpled white rose from her bag. As she stands, she lays it in the warm flattened grass where we lay. Then she's walking away, her back too stiff, her shoulders too high, and I'm stretched thin: snagged in her heart, fixed to that place – stretched, keening, snapped back.

'It's a ship,' I say with a burst of joy.

'A ship,' Beth murmurs.

And the June sky blazes.

'I've missed you,' I say.

'I miss you,' she says watching the slow changing clouds; ever changing, never changing clouds.

Bluebells

The scent of bluebells – intoxicating – a green smell – turns my stomach, and the sight of the shimmering blue carpet chokes me. But I'm drawn to these woods at this time of year and have been for forty years. I hope this will be the last time.

My hands slip, sweaty on the steering wheel, and the familiar tight band is squeezing my chest. Sunlight flickers over the windshield as the woods begin to enfold the road. Bella, my Springer Spaniel, is bouncing about the boot, sniffing enthusiastically between the bars that keep her from bouncing over me. She sucks in the scented draft from my open window, hoovering up April, the woods, new growth, the stench of bluebells. A familiar section of stone wall at a turn in the lane; beyond, the woods will surround this stretch of road, a vista of blue on either side. This place is famous for bluebells and people come from miles around to see them. I came a long way too. I moved away three decades ago but never miss my annual pilgrimage: I owe it to Fran.

Even though I'm expecting it, as I round the bend, the powder-blue, deep-blue, undulating sea of flowers makes my head spin. Then the sight is blocked as the road dips between Cotswold stone walls. I'm gripping the steering wheel and holding my breath, my heart stuttering in my ribs like a moth in a lantern. And, like the moth, I feel my life may suddenly snuff out – frazzle – sizzle – and I'll cease to be – wishful thinking, perhaps.

Parking up, I let Bella loose into the woods and, with a deep breath, follow her in. It's bright, the path only shadowed with a tracery of bare branches. The trees are still in bud with, here and there, an occasional splash of livid green as a sapling attempts to maximise the spring light before being over-shadowed by its parent. I can sympathise. My mother died when I was five and Fran, my sister, was three, so we were brought up by my father. He was a historian, well thought of – published – and he had high expectations for us. He also had high moral values, especially in relation to girls, and never tired of lecturing us on the wickedness of the world and what it would do to us given the chance. Fran and I were close, allies; and would escape the strict regime of home life whenever we could. Escape into the countryside, the woods around our home, the worlds we conjured from our imaginations: our safe places.

In our young minds, the return of the bluebells signified hope, escape, lengthening days. The bells, fragile and tremulous, spoke to our tender souls and the hovering otherworldly haze of blue was the perfect backdrop to our innocent fantasies. We peopled the woods with fairytales. We saw pixies and brownies creep from mossy logs, gossamer fairies skimmed the flowers, delighting in the ringing bells that only they and we could hear. A woodpecker was the tap of a dwarf fashioning treasure. A breeze heralded the swift charge of a prince on horseback; a mound was a dragon; gnarled roots hid a goblin; a ruinous pile of stones was haunted by a witch; wicked kings and evil uncles stalked the undergrowth; monsters waited in dark places. But innocence ends; usually slowly, gradually, due to the steady insistence of reality, the drudgery of daily life; usually slowly… but not always. Sometimes it's gone in a moment: a moment that pins you to itself; fixes you to a place and time however much your life flows on. Holds you there – binds you.

Bella has raced away and is barking out of sight. I whistle to her; there's somewhere we're headed, a place I have to get to, a place that fills me with dread: a place that draws and repels me. She streaks back, crashing past, pounding feet, streaming ears, lolling tongue, glancing up; a glimpse of the whites of her eyes, blurred movement, racing joyfully ahead down the familiar path. Fran ran ahead that day too. She always did – always.

'Fran, wait...' Her thin legs flash white way down the stippled path; a long way away. 'Wait for me!'
'I'll be the Queen of the castle and you're the dirty rascal,' she sings back.
We're headed for our favourite place, our secret place: the centre of our imaginary world – a high ring of bumpy mounds deep in the woods. Father says it's an old fort from long ago; to us it's a palace, the entrance to fairyland, ships sailing the bluebell sea, the green hump-backs of whales. In the centre where the land dips like a bowl we've made a shelter – dragging and stacking branches; weeks of work – a sanctuary: our Eeyore house of sticks. It's Saturday and we have the whole day. I made peanut butter sandwiches and we have cans of fizzy orange, apples, and sherbet fountains. I try to catch her up but the plastic bag of food and essential equipment – like the string of glass beads that once belonged to mother, and the spyglass made from toilet rolls – is heavy and awkward. It bangs on my legs and cuts into my hand. Fran doesn't have a bag. She always says we'll share carrying, but we never do. I don't mind really, she's only little. I'm ten and bigger than her and always look out for her, always.
She's already left the path and is toiling up the steep climb to our secret camp. I follow, carefully picking through the bluebells: I can't bear to hurt a single one, I love them;

they're so delicate and beautiful, so easy to crush. It takes so much concentration to climb the hill and carry the bag, and not step on the flowers, that I don't realise I can't see Fran anymore. I'm nearly at the top and I stop to say something but she's not there.

'Fran?'

'Shhhhh…'

I can't see her at first; she's at the top of the slope crouched in a tangled fringe of wild clematis – old man's beard. She's peering down into our secret dell. I drop the bag and, in a half crouch and as quietly as I can, scramble into the hiding place beside her.

'There's someone in our camp,' she breathes in my ear, her breath smells of cornflakes and milk.

I part the screen of dangling stalks, some thick as Tarzan vines, and have a look. I see a hunched-over shape. They're wearing a greasy mackintosh.

'It's a man,' whispers Fran.

'I can see that!'

'What's he doing in our camp?'

'How should I know?'

'He's going to spoil everything, make him go away.'

I look back at the man. How do you make a grown up go away, how do you stop them spoiling everything? Fran is looking at me, waiting for me to sort it out, like I always do, always.

'Let's get round to the other side,' I say. 'We can see what he's up to from there.'

The man looks like a tramp with lank hair sticking to his head and a grizzled beard. It also looks like he's slept in our shelter – how disgusting – how dare he? We crouch behind a thick oak on the far side of the dell to watch him. We've found the big sticks we had last week for magic

33

staves. They were just where we'd left them. I feel more confident now we have them. The tramp is bending over a fire, heating something in a blackened can; a thin spiral of smoke as blue as the spring woods, trails into the bare canopy, showing dark against the bright sky.

'What's he doing?' whispers Fran.

'Having breakfast.'

'What's he eating?'

'How should I know?'

'Has he killed something and skinned it?

'No.'

'Tell him to go away.'

She looks directly at me, her face full of confidence in my ability to sort it out, sort everything out.

'What if he's dangerous?' I say.

'Like a murderer?'

'Yes.'

'I think he's a wicked goblin… and he eats little girls.'

'I can hear you whispering,' says the man.

He doesn't look away from his pot; just stirs it and blows on the smoke, but he knows we're here! We duck further behind the tree. Fran is staring at me, wide eyed, hugging her knees. I can feel my heart racing and banging about.

'Come on out, lads – guess I'm using your camp – would like to see who I've got to thank for their hospitality.'

'We're not boys!'

Fran stands up, hands on hips, and frowns down at the man. That's done it. I join her and stand a bit in front in case there's trouble. I clutch my stick real tight.

'Girls, eh?'

He chuckles and carries on stirring. It sounds like a secret laugh, all to himself. I don't like him. I know better than Fran what men can do. Maybe he *is* a goblin like she says. That would be better: goblins can be vanquished.

'Why don't you come join me? I won't bite you.'

He looks straight at us and grins. His teeth are the colour of tea, and one of his eyes is funny. I put an arm out to stop Fran but she hasn't moved. I can feel her shaking.

'Suit yourselves,' he goes back to his stirring. 'Not exactly Prince Charming am I?'

So he is a goblin then, or maybe a wicked magician: grown ups don't talk about fairytales.

'This is *our* camp,' says Fran.

'S'pose you wish I'd go away?' he says, looking at me.

'Yes,' I say.

He keeps looking at me, his eyes narrow slits. Then he shrugs and goes back to his stirring. 'Not till I've had me breakfast.'

Silence stretches out. I don't know what to do. Fran nudges me in the back, but I still don't know what to do.

'Shame you ain't friendly – not a bad camp for a couple o'girls…'

He glances at me, it's a sly look. I won't take the bait. But Fran pushes past me and is half way down the slope before I can stop her.

'It's the best camp! Better than a boy's,' she says.

'Well, maybe it is. My apologies, M'Lady, and I thank y'kindly for the comfort of your lodgings.'

He gets up and gives Fran a bow. She giggles. I race after her and grab her arm – hold her back. It's a trap. The goblin-man looks at me for a long time, then goes back to his can. It's making a sizzling noise and the smoke from under it has gone black. He tuts and knocks it away from the fire with a stick.

'Is it burnt? What're you eating?' Fran leans against me, she's stopped shaking and her body feels warm on my bare arm.

'Beans and yes.' He starts to scoop the beans into his mouth with a black spoon out of his pocket. He huffs and blows on the scalding food; steam comes out of his mouth like smoke.

'Did you sleep in our Eeyore house?'

Fran pushes away from me. Why does she always have to ask things?

'I'm going to do it too,' she says slipping and clambering down the last part of the slope. 'Were you cold? Did you see any badgers? Did the Moon Elves come out?'

The goblin-man laughs, 'Moon Elves?'

'Yes, they come out on a full moon – was it a full moon? They dance like this...'

Fran drops her stick and starts to leap and spin like we do when we're on our own. I feel angry: this is our stuff, it's not for grown ups! She catches her foot and goes down smack on her face near the fire. I know it hurts because she just lies there. The man throws his tin away and jumps up. NO. I'm running down the slope swinging my stick; shouting: he mustn't touch her; I won't let him touch her. My stick hits him and there's the sound like you get when a coconut is knocked off the shy and the jolt goes up my arm. The stick spins away. The man falls down. I run to Fran.

The man hasn't moved. Fran has stopped crying but her nose is running and she shudders when she breathes. I've tied my hanky round the cut on her knee. He still hasn't moved.

'Is he dead?' She looks at me, white-faced, tear-streaked, afraid.

I go and stand over the man. I poke him with my stick. There's blood matting his greasy hair. He doesn't move or make a noise or breathe.

'You killed him,' whispers Fran. 'You killed a man.'

'Not a man … it's a goblin. It was going to get you.' I want to believe this real bad. There's a hollow place in my middle and my legs are wobbly. 'It was a wicked goblin.'

Fran's shaking. 'Yes, he had brown teeth, all goblins have brown teeth.' Her own teeth are chattering. 'What shall we do? Do we need to call the police?'

'NO. They wouldn't understand. And grown ups can't see goblins. We have to send it back to where it came from.'

'How?'

'Hide—bury it.'

'In our Eyore house?'

'No, at the base of the ring: it can get straight back to fairyland from there.'

It took the whole day. I remember how we toiled, scraping the dry earth with sticks, rocks, our hands. The man was heavy. We rolled him and covered him with his blanket and placed his things in with him: a burnt tin of beans, a black spoon. Fran picked bluebells and dropped them in too; they scattered across his stained bedding, fresh against soiled cloth. The grave wasn't deep – but it was never found. I've been waiting all my life for it to be found.

The days following the burial, I was convinced the police would come to the house, talk with father, take me away. I half wanted it, but it never happened. No-one was reported missing. As the days turned to weeks, I tried to convince myself he'd been a goblin after all, I tried to convince Fran. She agreed but we both knew it was a lie. We were never close again: I had failed her. She turned to father for comfort; absolution. She got more love than she bargained for and that was my fault too: I should have stopped her – stopped him. But I never could.

Fran took her own life on her twenty-first birthday.

I've reached the top of the fort. The blue woods shimmer all around me. Down in the dell our shelter is long gone, but over the years others have replaced it and been replaced themselves: it's still a favourite place for a camp – a secret camp – a secret. I come here every year. The anniversary of the day I killed him; the man who slept in our camp and who ruined our lives – guilt and resentment. Some years I've hated him, some years I've been sorry, always filled with loathing – for that moment, for me, him, father, Fran. But today will be the end of it: the day I unstick myself; the day I send the goblin packing; send all the demons packing. Father is dead and the academic world has finished its eulogies and turned back to its books. There's no reason to hide anymore, there's no reason to keep anything hid – it can *all* come out.

The quiet, birdsong woods are shattered by a burst of static and a tinny synthetic voice. Down on the path, dark and bulky with Kevlar vest, a policeman fiddles with his radio, looks up at me, nods, and speaks into his shoulder, speaks to the tinny voice. He's found me. It's a shock to see a one of the boys in blue here after so long – funny, they're more black than blue, especially set against the trembling sapphire carpet all around – a shock after all the years of secrets and silence, a shock even though I called and asked them to come. My mouth is dry. Bella senses my unease and settles on my foot, growling at the approaching man – the black and white solidity huffing up the bank – my nightmare – my delivering angel. As he climbs his shining boots plough the bluebells, crushing their delicate fragility, destroying them with the weight of his presence. Every step up the bank an obliteration; an end to the blue goblins that torment my soul, and the start of spring.

The Fox and the Moon

Fox knew how handsome he was; from the rough taste of his flank as he smoothed his russet fur, to the sight of his thick bush of a tail, to the deep musk of his scent. No other was as bold and as brave and as clever as he. No hen house could keep him out, no goose could chase him from her eggs, no rabbit could out run him: Fox was the lord of the meadows, the master of hedgerow and copse, the king of the silent wood.

One soft spring night Fox woke and shook his musky self out of his den. Hunger gnawed his belly and, as he looked up and saw the moon, hunger twisted his heart with love.

'Come down, beloved,' he called, 'and be my wife.'

The moon shone achingly bright, then drew a cloud over her beauty and dropped a deluge of spring rain. Fox chuckled, shook himself, and trotted into the April shower in search of dinner.

Later, belly full, Fox picked his way through an old hollow way, silver light once again shining down striping the path. 'Come, beloved,' Fox whispered and, all of a sudden as he slipped past a rain filled rut, he caught a glimpse of his love beside him: a flash of silver across the puddle. Then she was gone, back out of reach above the tracery of uncurling leaves.

Fox trotted on his heart beating fast.

He jumped a waterlogged ditch and for a moment she was with him again. Then she was before him. He ran on, down to the lake where she was waiting for him.

Fox leapt onto his beloved.

With a splash he disappeared beneath the cold water, his lady scattering into a million drops and ripples. All night long Fox swam the silver tracks of the lake, his heart's desire always breaking and shimmering away around him, till the moon began to dip to the west and the waters darkened.

Exhausted, Fox dragged himself out of the water. His heart was breaking. Why had his lady teased him so? Then, up in the copse on the top of the hill, silver light flamed through the trees.

She was come.

Tired as he was, Fox pushed through the hedgerow and started up the hill to be with his beloved at last. If he hadn't been so tired he might have used his wiles to go by secret ways. If he hadn't been so focussed on his love he might have been more cautious.

The farmer's boy rubbed sleep from his eyes on that early April morn and squinted down the barrel of his gun. He could barely believe what he saw: Fox slap bang in full view!

He squeezed the trigger.

Who would mourn Fox?
Not the chickens in their house.
Not the goose on her eggs.
Not the rabbit in the meadow.
Not the farmer patting his fat boy.
Only the moon mourns Fox as she waits alone in the silent copse.

The Misty Aisle

'Freezer six is playing up.' Sheena totters from breakfast cereals on inappropriately high heels and slumps behind her till. 'Smoke's comin' out. You'll have to sort it, Derick, before the bloody thing kills us. I ain't goin' to sit here an' be gassed or blown up. I'll bloody sue if I am.'

'How will you manage that, Sheena, if you're dead? And please remember to address me as Mr Trip, I *am* the manager,' says Derick Trip.

'That last trainin' day they said how we was to call each other by our first names – Derick.'

Sheena stares at Mr Trip chewing her gum, daring him to disagree. He remains silent. One eye twitches and his face goes a darker shade of red. Sheena blows an enormous bubble that pops across her chin.

'Do your uniform up please, Sheena, this is not Saturday night down the Bell and Garter,' says Mr Trip. 'I can see your ... it's not descen— just do it up!'

He turns on his heel, takes a deep breath and straightens his tie before heading for aisle three. Behind him, Gary – carrying a box of super-soft toilet tissue – lumbers up to Sheena.

'You alright, Shee? That old pervert lookin' at your tits again? Want me to sort 'im out?'

'Nah, prob'ly the only thrill 'e gets. 'E was on about callin' 'im Mr Trip, pompous twat.'

'Mr Tits, more like,' says Gary. They both laugh.

Derick sighs and marches into the relative haven of aisle three – jams, condiments and breakfast products – away from the petty, stupid, disrespectful, childish ... he takes a deep breath. It's up to him to mould his young workforce, show them the way; just as Mr Abbott had for him all those years ago at Grace and Nobles. Ah, Grace and Nobles, now that had been a fine shop! No first names there. Even at the closing down party he'd called everyone by their proper title. He's still proud he never knew their first names. Twenty years, for what? To become the manager of a low-cost food store. He sighs again.

Fog rolls around his ankles, obscuring his neat shoes. It's coming from freezer six. Dense, cold vapour filling the aisle like milk in a glass. He leans on the freezer to shut it, it makes no difference. He heaves the lid open and is engulfed in a cloud. It has a faint smell, reminding him of something he can't quite put his finger on; sunlight, if that can have a smell. He remembers running through buttercups as a child without his shoes and socks on, and how the sun felt and the air tasted. He slams the lid shut but the vapour pours out ever thicker. Under the foggy plastic top the contents glow. Derick snorts, smoothes his moustache and exits aisle three. He'll have to call maintenance.

The rest of the morning is very trying for Derick Trip. The aisle is off-limits to the public so he has to keep intercepting customers searching for breakfast commodities. Before the mist reached his chin he ventured in for them, but the last time he tried to fetch a jar of marmalade, he became lost and only got out by following the sound of Janice announcing the day's specials.

Unusually large numbers of people want aisle three today and some of them appear to be quite strange, even by budget foodstore standards. People must be slipping into the aisle from the other end: there are muffled voices and shadowy figures. They could be pocketing goods! He hesitates on the edge of the vapour before thrusting his head in. 'Any shoppers in aisle three please exit at once. This is for your own safety. I have staff stationed at both ends to assist you.' No response, but faintly, on the edge of hearing, he catches the sound of a fiddle.

'I'm sorry madam but I can't let you go in,' says Mr Trip, exasperation mounting, his comb-over flapping free. 'It's for your own safety, there's a fault with one of the freezers and you may become disorientated and injure yourself.'
The little old lady in tweed smiles. 'Do you know what day it is?' she says.
Mr Trip shrugs. What had that got to do with anything?
'It's Lammas, dear,' she says, poking him with her brolly to get him to move.
Mr Trip stays resolute. After poking him a few more times she gives up. He can't be sure but he thinks her fox-fur stole winks as she disappears into Baking in aisle two.
'All right?' says Janice, coming out of two carrying a box of eggs.
'That old lady's collar was alive? Did you see?' Mr Trip tries to rearrange his hair. He likes Janice, she's always respectful.
'What old lady?' Janice looks concerned. 'You've been at this all day, why don't you take a break, have a sit down?'
Mr Trip's irritation builds. Why is Janice speaking to him like he's an idiot?
'I'll bring you a nice cup of tea,' she says, and hastily adds, 'you can keep an eye on aisle three on the CCTV.'
That's it! The footage will show them getting into the aisle. He laughs and hurries across the shop, doing his best to ignore Sheena and Gary. She makes a gesture to indicate that he, Mr Trip, is mad, then tries to turn it into innocent hair twiddling. They're laughing at him. He'll

deal with them later; right now there are more important things to do.

Odd: he's gone over and over the footage and it doesn't make sense.

Janice puts a hot cup of tea in front of him and picks up the untouched one. 'Please try and have something,' she says. 'You haven't touched your Garibaldi, I opened the packet special.'

'I can't find the old lady ... or the dwarf ... or that tall gentleman with the dogs!' Mr Trip jabs at the keyboard, fast forwarding the film for the umpteenth time. 'And if they did get into aisle three, I haven't seen them coming out. Have they been through the tills yet?'

'Haven't seen anyone like that, coming in or going out,' says Janice, 'Please drink your tea, Mr Trip. The last one went cold.'

She tip-toes out, closing the door quietly as if afraid of startling him. Derick bends over the monitor. He'll go through the footage frame by frame if he has to! On the film he's clearly talking to people, but they aren't showing up. The equipment is obviously faulty. He rings headquarters, reports the defective cameras and explains in some detail the difficulties he's having due to the broken freezer. He's told not to worry, they're sure he is doing his best and tomorrow they'll send an engineer. Mr Trip goes back to his monitor.

He jumps as Sheena barges in. 'It's gone half five, Derick,' she says. 'We're off; you'd better lock up.'

The door bangs behind her. Mr Trip shuts down his computer, turns everything off at the plugs and locks the office. The shop is quiet except for the low hum of freezers. He checks the rear doors, turns off the lights and is on his way to the automatic door at the front when he notices a light still on: it's coming from aisle three.

A freezer must be open. He knew people had been mucking about in there! Ducking under the security tape, he blunders toward freezer number six. He leans on the lid but the light remains on. Funny, looks like there are *lots* of lights. He puts his ear to the frosty surface – music – lovely and lively. It makes him yearn for summer and flowers and no shoes and socks and his lost youth. He lifts the lid. Wild strains of a reel wash over him as he climbs inside.

Never before has Derick Trip seen such wonders or danced with such abandon. The meadow is as he remembered, except the buttercups seem brighter and the sky a darker blue set with stars. They're all there; the little old lady, the dwarf, the tall man with his hounds, and many more; all beautiful and merry and somehow terrible. There's food and treasures: jewels, silver, and great chunks of gold. One lump and he could leave the budget food industry behind forever – say good-bye to the petty wrangling and disrespect – tell head office to shove their pension scheme and their training days and their modern ways where Sunny Delight doesn't shine!

When Sheena arrives next morning, the mist has gone and everything is back to normal: everything except for Mr Trip's tie poking out from freezer number six.

When he's defrosted and they've prised open his stiff fingers; they find a crispy coated chicken nugget clutched fiercely to his breast. The coroner brings in a verdict of suicide following a mental breakdown. But no-one can explain the smile on Derick Trip's face or the buttercup pollen between his toes.

Little Brown Mouse

Little brown mouse hunkers down, quivering beneath the dock leaves, as a shadow circles the field: hawk is hunting for her dinner.
Little mouse waits.
The shadows soften, fading, till the dark menace moving across the grass is altogether gone.
Mouse creeps from her shelter.
And hawk gets her meal.
Being so tiny, little brown mouse had no concept of the sky or how clouds steal shadows away.

Tam Lin

'What?' I can't hear him over the pulsing sound. Around us the club heaves; a sweaty throbbing entity. He signals the barmaid and two shots slide over ink-dark, slop strobing with neon. He chinks my glass and downs his drink. My heart quivers. I imagine his pale flesh under my lips, the taste of him. The crowd shifts, squeezing our bodies together; his arm slips round me as he leans in, mouth on my ear, to breathe his name.

In the forest, a maiden, fair, fresh and scented with heather, tarries at a well. She sings as she plucks a wild rose; a song of longing; a song of love. A pale knight, tall and lean with eyes dark and soft as the night, steps out of the trees: the elfin guardian of the wood. No maiden returns unscathed from an encounter with this wan spirit but Janet is unafraid. She lingers as the sun glides through the sky, wrapped in the wood's mossy musk, trapped by the silky embrace of love. As the day ends in burning orange, she leaves the forest a maid no more.

Hard flesh, taught and white, my skin pink against his pallor; our shuddering union consumes the night, tipping into the grey dawn.
He reaches through empty cans and moulding mugs to find a crumpled packet of fags. Flame and ash and reek of smoke; his sharp cheekbones serrate my heart, his caress dimples my soul. I trace the waxen beauty of his inner arm, stroke the line of it, the lines on it; livid and red.

'Save me,' he says, cupping my full flushed breast in his bony fingers; drawing the beat of my blood against his cool ribs. 'Save me.'

Janet returns to her lover's embrace day after day and they whisper their longing, bathe in the wonder of the other's gaze. His name is Tam Lin and is as mortal as she. Once, in the past, he tells her, he was enthralled by the unearthly beauty of the Fae Queen and was captured. Now he is bound to her service: by day he guards the wood, by night he rides in her cavalcade; her favourite knight; an unwilling slave. But Janet can save him if she has strength and courage – if her love is true.

What can he offer: an intoxicating life, a life of intoxication; wild hedonism, and sensual indulgence; life a step to the side of every day? What can I offer: hope of escape?
The allure of the club wears thin. Denizens ground in the jaws of its High Court. I tire of its jaded officials, its fading victims. The novelty is crushed by repetition and I see my pale love longs to turn his face to the sun: is waiting for salvation.
But hope is fragile. Flimsy as cigarette papers, fleeting as chopped out lines; snort and slaver, drag and puff; ash and dust on the wind.

She knows what to do: Mid-night, Allhallows Eve, she waits at a crossroads to see the Fairy host pass. Luminous creatures of starlight, delicate as the gossamer wings of moths, heady as night scented stock, strange as the moon: the Queen and her entourage trip and jingle out of the forest, and step lightly down the road. Janet waits for her

50

pale knight astride his star-bright stallion, then leaps and encircles his waist, dragging him from his mount.

A clinic of cracked lino and sterile air – promises are rainbow bubbles in sunlight – substitute chemicals – resentment. I struggle to hold him from the baying courtiers; glittering and vibrant by night; bloated and sallow by day; they suck at his soul and whisper their poison-laced enticements: tempting and cajoling.
His dull eyes turn to the wall and I stroke his shivering frame; wrap it in my hot flesh; press the bright quivering spark of life that stirs within me against his sweat, slick back; a beacon. 'Come home,' I whisper to the dark.

The Fae Queen shrieks at the betrayal, eyes raging, focused on Tam Lin. Janet feels her lover cool and slither; a serpent in her arms, writhing, coiling, and crushing; but she holds on. He swells and bellows, rank odour, raking claws, teeth in her flesh: a bear in her embrace, but Janet tightens her grip. Fur stiffens and form stretches, wings beating the night, hard beak stabbing: her lover a violent, hissing swan, but her love for him transcends the pain. The Queen cries with fury, shrill and piercing. The tumult abates and Tam Lin's monstrous form contracts, the weight and agony almost too much, Janet staggers: a bar of iron, incandescent with heat is clutched to her heart. This is the last test and she must act.

Real monsters use their fists.

Mortal flesh burning Janet shuts out the screaming host of the fae as they wheel about her. She runs to the forest and the well. Amid the maelstrom of wrath, she hurls the searing metal into the water. Steam erupts into the night.

Silence. The unearthly gathering melts away in the vapour, all save the Queen; beautiful and cold, she surveys her rival.

'If I had known that mortal love could take my knight, I would have ripped out his heart and replaced it with stone,' she says, and is gone.

Tam Lin steps naked and pure from the depths of the well and Janet enfolds him in her cloak – wraps him in love.

Life is no fairytale. At best it's a truce with the circling demons; a tremulous pact, brittle and transient.

I snatch moments to hoard against a lost future. Catch them in the tender net of my longing. They float through my thoughts, bright islands, isolated flashes: our child touching my lover's smile; warmth in his dark eyes; a pale cheek flushing; laughter. I treasure them like a miser; images as fleeting as blossom on a spring breeze or the soft blooming of a bruise.

Is my love strong enough to hold him; is my love strong enough to be saved? The club still heaves and sweats behind the anonymity of a scarred, heavy door; heaves and waits and reels in the line.

The Jewellery Mat

The old jeweller spreads out his soft leather mat and waits. He strokes the pale oval fondly. The mat never leaves him. He says it brings out the lustre in gold, makes silver shine, enhances any jewel. Sandy dust blows in through the plastic curtains hung to delineate his work space. Periodically he brushes it off the mat. After a while a shadow moves outside and a man ducks through the entrance. He has come to get a good price for his gold.

They come to the old jeweller to sell their precious possessions, family heirlooms, old treasured trinkets. Gold, silver, jewels – he weighs and appraises and offers credit tokens for them. He is not the only buyer in the market district but most come to him, especially those loathed to part with their goods; those who feel that this last sale is a betrayal. They come because he shows courtesy. There is etiquette to the transaction; dignity. And he tells them a tale of his lost love as a distraction, as compensation. The man sits cross-legged, shifting self-consciously. He draws a small bag from his hazmat coverall and drops it onto the mat.

The jeweller has seen all the ways customers choose to reveal their goods: some lay each object out with care; others pour it from a rattling box; many toss over a bag or rolled rag as if it has little consequence to them; a few keep it in their hand, reluctant to part with it into another's grasp. However they arrive, the jeweller treats the goods the same: carefully separating and arranging them on his soft pale leather mat; his small oval arena. Then he makes tea. He can only spare a few dry flakes to make the brew and there is no milk or lemon but he always has a little sugar if his customers wish for it. Not real sugar of course – since the ban and collapse of the sugar trade it has become as rare as a litre of petrol or as scarce as a kept promise – but the synthetic block he owns is a good substitute.

With slow deliberation, the jeweller arranges the trinkets on his mat. Times have been bad for a long age. The flood of people with quality items reduced to a trickle and then a drip; and now come the desperate with mostly worthless junk. But the ritual is still the same. One by one the objects are placed on the mat; a worn ring; a broken fragment of chain; a silver thimble. Now he makes tea as carefully as he laid out the goods, and hands a cracked china cup to his customer. They sip the steaming liquid in silence for a while before the jeweller fits a glass to his eye and bends to his work.

He holds up the ring worn wafer-thin by generations. 'It's gold,' he muses 'and much loved. I gave a similar thing to my beloved many years ago…'

The customer settles down with his tea. This is as he expected.

'She had skin as luminous as the moon,' says the jeweller, regarding his customer through the gold band; 'and as soft as thistledown scented with wild broom.'

The tale unfolds as the jeweller sorts, tests, weighs and appraises. Afterwards customers have difficulty remembering the details, except the lover had skin bright as the moon and as soft as thistledown. They leave the booth with far fewer credits than they had hoped for, should have expected. But the tale of longing woven with fragrant tea and the gentle voice of the jeweller, always worked its magic.

The jeweller lays down the last item and runs his hands over the pale surface of the mat. The story was told, the tea drunk, the deal done and a price agreed. They shake hands. The customer leaves the booth like one emerging from a dream.

Sandy dust blows through the curtain. The jeweller brushes it off the leather mat. The mat that is as soft as broom-scented thistledown and as luminous as the moon.

AI

Stop. Breathe. Calm yourself you idiot. It'll be monitoring heat signatures and oxygen usage. I need to reduce my consumption; mask my location. I take a long breath and try to slow my heart: being in a state of near panic is not helpful. The corridor sweeps out of sight. I'm in the inner link-ring of the ship and have to find my way to comms on the other side – call for help, or at least alert others of the takeover. They need to send a clean-up squad before we dock with a hub. The ship judders and I feel momentarily light then weighed down as the anti-grav adjusts to flight mode. The ignition sequence always makes me nauseous and faint. I have to steady myself against the nearest bulkhead and lean my forehead against the cool smoothness of a view-port. Within the ships rings the gyroscopic drive-mechanism has started its spin. It's already a blur and will soon pass beyond human vision as it reaches maximum push. Where's the bastard taking us?

I am Trant, Juno Trant, first mate on the earth led galaxy-class science ship The Beagle and I think I may be the only surviving member of our crew. Eleven earth days ago we docked at Delta-17 in the Andromeda section, a trade port under the jurisdiction of the earth alliance, to take on supplies and have a little well earned R and R; but we left with more than we bargained for. Somehow the ship was infected with a rogue AI. Things got nasty really quickly. Systems started to malfunction however much we purged them. It baffled our Tech guys. Security firewalls and failsafe routines are hardwired into the mainframe to protect against just such an attack but nothing seemed to work. Every time a system was cleared, another went down. Then the crew started to act crazy. It began with fever and irrational behaviour but quickly escalated to self-harm, suicide, violence. People let themselves out of air-locks, mutilated themselves, turned on one another then blew their own brains out. It happened fast and it was unstoppable. How the AI affected behaviour, I still haven't worked out… they can't infect bio's…?

Five centuries ago we developed artificial intelligence and it almost lead to our annihilation. AI evolved exponentially and before we could halt its progress it had turned on us. The resulting war was going badly for us till the intervention of – what we termed then – extraterrestrials. It would seem that the galaxies beyond our own were not keen on the prospect of AI's rampaging across the known universes. We joined the inter-galaxy alliance and in exchange for their help we had to sign up to the total destruction of all forms of non-sanctioned artificial intelligence. It was, in effect, a form of genocide. A few units survived and slipped into exile. They are hunted with extreme prejudice and summarily terminated. It means that those still out there evolve ever more cunning ways to evade detection and we have to develop more and more extreme measures to eradicate them. All life forms want to survive: contact with them is, therefore, deadly.

'Juno? Cap? Anyone?'

The voice echoes along the empty corridor: it's coming from a comm-port just out of sight round the curve; it sounds like Frattelli, the ship's medic. Jesus, I thought everyone was dead! My heart pounds as I skid to a stop at the wall-mounted unit and fumble with the keypad.

'Tel? Is that you? You OK? I thought—' I choke up and have to swallow hard before I can trust myself to speak again. 'Where the hell are you? NO, wait, don't say, *it*'s in all the ship's systems, it'll be monitoring the comms. It'll have our locations now from the link we're using.'

'I'll go to the place you'd expect to find me at this time of evening,' he says.

The gym, Frattelli's a health nut and works out for two hours every evening. 'Ok,' I say, 'meet you there. Don't use the links again or try to access any of the systems…and that includes the equipment in there, it's linked to the central computer and that's been compromised. See you shortly.'

Knowing someone else is alive gives me hope, I just pray he's not been affected. The thought brings the memory of all the violence and madness crashing back in. I've done a good job of suppressing it till now. Anger boils over. Bastard bloody machine! My gun is in my hand and I'm firing and firing, blasting the comm. unit – repeatedly. Christ! Am I loosing it too – is this how it starts? I force myself to re-holster my firearm and wait till I've mastered my emotions.

Sparks shoot from the comm. unit and, with a final 'whump', it explodes, filling the place with dense smoke. All that's left is a charred hole, fizzing with dangling wires. The fire alarm shrieks throughout the ship, amber lights flashing through the haze and with grim satisfaction I aim at the nearest security camera and take that out too. After all the running and hiding I've been doing for the past few hours, this feels good. It may be suicidal; the biggest here-I-am-come-get-me I could have managed but, to be honest, I think the ship has been monitoring me all along. At least this way, if I can take out some of the surveillance units, I might create a section of ship without sensors that Tel and I can hide in; a sanctuary till help arrives.

The gym is three bulkheads along and one up. Through the next set of doors is a crewman, I think its Collins, difficult to tell as most of his face is missing. He's slumped awkwardly in a cabin doorway. I check for life but he's obviously been dead some time; it's not obvious what killed him, but it did a thorough job. The security cameras and any computer terminals get the brunt of my wroth. I even blast the door locks and food dispensers; anything that might have a link to central hub. Prising open a weapons locker, I grab more ammo, a spare blaster, and an emergency backpack. How this will help against an AI Unit I'm not really sure but it makes me feel better, more prepared.

Up through a service hatch, via a metal ladder to the next level: the main habitation and recreation zone. I'm straight into a large open concourse with windows facing outward. I try to get my bearings, see which direction the ship's headed, but unless there's something within close proximity, it's impossible to tell: the stars are simply too far away to discern movement with the naked eye. This sector is a vast empty void of space. I have to get to Ops.

The next set of doors stays locked. Shit! The hub is beginning to work against me. No matter, since the Tech War, manual over-rides were fitted to *everything!* It's why the bastard AI hasn't been able to turn off the life-support or gravity systems: they run on good old-fashioned mechanical engines.

The fire alarm cuts out.

Silence except for my ragged breathing. Reel it in Juno, remember your training. Crossing the rec. hall, it's as if the crew just rushed out: plates of half eaten congealed food litter the tables, overturned cups are stuck in hardened pools of coffee, beer, whatever... there's blood on the back of one of the chairs. The hatch through to the galley is blackened with fire damage: guess someone put a pan on before they went nuts. One more stop before the gym – I want to swap these firearms with their micro-chips and programming for something a little more traditional – something an AI won't be able to affect.

The locker room is filled with steam. Glancing into the showers, there's a body, pink and glistening, under the scorching water. My locker is badly dented, damaged by some sort of struggle; there's no-one in here; the folded clothes of the crewman in the showers looks incongruous in its neat pile on the bench. I have to jimmy the locker door. Inside is my crossbow.

The gym appears empty, silent. Maybe Tel hasn't made it yet, maybe he won't...

'You took your time.'

I spin round. Tel is leaning against the wall beside the door. I'm getting sloppy, forgetting the basics; if he was a hostile I'd be dead now!

'Jesus, you gave me a fright.' My heart's racing, I'm sweaty and dishevelled; I must look in sharp contrast to Tel: he's neat, collected, calm. Too calm; something's off. There's a second exit to the room but it's blocked with fallen equipment – shit! Tel comes toward me hands outstretched as if to ... what? Hug me, shake my hand? I side-step, I've got a firearm resting casually over the crook of my arm. I check the safety is off. Tel shrugs and walks on past, tapping me lightly on the arm as he does. The gesture is reassuring – human, and I feel a little guilty for not trusting him but can't shake off the warning bells either. Tel stops in the centre of the room, I've got the door to my back now – better – I slow my breathing and smile at him.

'Anyone else made it?' I say.

'Just you and me.'

A chill runs through me. 'Well, Doc, what's your assessment – why'd everyone go crazy?'

Tel inclines his head as if thinking. He glances at my arm and I realise I'm scratching the place he touched. I stop, not wanting him to think his contact was unwelcome. The area tingles slightly. He smiles.

'No sign of any pathogen or poisoning. I was able to examine one crewman before he threw himself out of an airlock and there were some abnormalities in his brain wave pattern – not unusual in a psychosis.'

'Brought on by what? And how come the whole crew was affected?'

'Mass psychosis is not unknown in situations of extreme stress—'

'Bullshit!'

Tel doesn't react to my interruption except to incline his head again. I never knew the man well, but enough to know he's not behaving as he should. On closer scrutiny his breathing is too regular; his posture too upright, even his blinking is uniform. I raise the firearm and level it at his chest.

'Sorry, Doc, but how do I know you haven't been affected? You don't seem yourself!'

He seems about to argue back then stops and grins. The expression is exaggerated and the smile wide enough to split his lower lip. A drop of blood beads and rolls onto his chin; he wipes it off and looks at his reddened fingers.

'Oops!' He looks up at me; his lip still bleeding; he ignores it. 'What gave me away? It's the nuances isn't it? You are a surprisingly complex life form.'

The skin prickles along my spine.

'Of course not all of you are compatible and I have to say my technique was somewhat clumsy to start with. I have learned from my mistakes, I'm good at that, and luckily there were lots of you.'

He – it, smiles again using only half of Tel's mouth. It feels Tel's face, pressing and moving the skin as if to mould it. 'Can't seem to get the smile right! Who would have thought it was such a difficult process?'

'How? How'd you get in us? Surgical implants?' I keep the gun trained on Tel's chest and check my exit is still clear.

'Oh, nothing so crude, I've developed a form of nanotech. I'm able to exist as a hive mind. I took my inspiration from Bees and ants. Insects are quite wonderful and you humans do your best to squash and kill them at every opportunity.'

'Not possible, the ship's sensors are calibrated to pick up nano-technology.'

'Not *my* tech. I make your nanos look like juggernauts! Mine are small enough to slip through atoms; enter cells. A single unit is as small as a virus – another life form you humans seek to destroy at every opportunity. And like a virus I have developed the ability to replicate.'

Oh, God, it must be everywhere!

The AI regards me intensely. 'I see from your expression that you are realising the futility of your situation. Yes, indeed I am everywhere.'

It laughs, the sound odd, contrived, filling me with revulsion. I pull the trigger. Tel staggers back against a press-bench, a hole in his chest. It puts a hand to the wound.

'You've broken the pump,' it says.

Tel's body slumps over the bench: lifeless.

I run in blind panic through the empty silence of the ship and end up in the vast hydroponic atria. It's where I always come if I'm troubled. It's the heart of the ship;

providing fresh food and oxygen, and enrichment for the soul. Think, Juno, think! The ship is lost – nowhere on board is safe and it's a matter of time till I'm infected. If somehow I can get the auto destruct to work, it'll send a cloud of nano AI's hurtling across space: an invisible ever expanding cloud that will infect anything in its path. No good – I have to get a message out. The ship has to be quarantined in a force sphere till our tech boys can figure out how to combat this. Ops, then – I have to make it to the bridge. I don't know how I'll bypass the AI's control or if I'll get there before it stops me but I'll have to try. It may not know of the emergency comm. unit, it's not wired into the main computer, and I may just have time to get something out before it infiltrates the circuitry. God, I have to hope so!

Ok, speed then; get it done before it works out what I'm up to. I'm going to use the service ducts and crawl spaces where there's no surveillance. It's a tighter space but I can take a few short cuts and direct links. Hopefully I'll be off grid till the last moment. I breathe the deep oxygen rich atmosphere and set off at a steady lope down the length of the verdant aisles, taking out cameras. At the far end, confident I've disabled all the surveillance – at least for the time being – I double back and drop through a trap door. I have to run in a half crouch; the space is low but stretches off in all directions, a few stray roots dangle from the roof, questing pointlessly for nutrients and water. The tendrils peter out and the space narrows as I pass out of the atria and into the accommodation block. Light levels are low but I know my way: up the ventilation shafts now to the top ring, six levels above.

'Juno, oh, Juno, where are you?' The soft female tones of the main computer echo down the duct: the AI is using ship-wide comms. 'Ah, there you are.'

A service drone hovers beside me. I lose my footing on the ladder reaching for my firearm but, even hanging by one hand, manage to put a shot in the machine. It tumbles away, crashing and bouncing from the walls.

'Spoilsport,' says the disembodied voice of the computer. 'What *are* you up to, scrabbling about in there?'

I ignore it and keep climbing. Two more levels then I'll have to sprint a short distance along the main corridor to the bridge.

'Isn't this fun? How about I set you another little dilemma … see what you do?'

Christ, I'm a rat in a maze to this bloody thing! Sight and sound cease. Pitch darkness; utter silence! I cling to the cold rung, disorientated in the sudden void, my breath coming in gasps; I can hear it, I'm not deaf then. The AI has cut the power: all power, including back-up. Unless it causes a breach, I've got about seven hours of air, but it's going to get cold; very cold. I strap a torch from the emergency pack to my wrist and continue climbing.

I make the bridge easily – too easily. What's the damn AI up to? I try to ignore the bodies, my crewmates. The emergency communicator is strapped under the main consol. It should be good to go: batteries are checked daily.

'Hey, Juno, whatcha doing.'

It's the AI. I turn and fire on the internal speaker system, taking out the camera at the same time.

'Not nice,' it says. The sound is tinny and small, coming from a personal communicator on the dead navigator's wrist. 'Maybe you'll be more disposed to like me if I use a different voice… how about this one? How y' doin' girl? Are y'missin' me?'

It's Cap's soft tones. The bastard machine is trying to mess with my head.

Y'heart rate's shot up there number one. Int'restin'. Y'know he's dead – he's right there in that chair beside you. Yet y'still have a response t' his voice. Hmmm, I'm learnin' such a lot from you, darlin'.'

'Stop it!'

'How about this voice then?'

It sounds like Carly; she stepped out of an airlock three days ago. I ignore it and focus on the task in hand. Switching on the comm. unit, I punch in the code for the combat-class ship The Elysey: it's the nearest vessel in this sector. Come on, come on…answer—

'Elysey – identify yourself?'

Thank God! 'Juno Trant, Alfa Gamma 47629, first mate, science ship The Beagle. Security code Delta 0010042 Omega 9.'

There's a crackle of static and then a familiar voice. 'Juno? It's Captain Emily Stewart here. Why are you on the emergency comms? What's happened?'

I feel a sting of tears at the sound of her voice: we were at the academy together and have stayed close since. 'AI takeover—'

'Holy Crap!'

'Ems, it's got nano technology. You have to quarantine the ship.'

'It's got what? Your signal's breaking up.'

'Nano-tech!'

'Not getting you; just static. Any casualties?'

'All dead – am the only one left.'

'Shit! Hang in there Ju. We've locked onto your location and will dock in a little under two hours.'

'NO! Keep your distance! Nano-technology will infect—'

'Just static… can you clean up the signal?' She's not talking to me.

'I'm doing the best I can,' the second voice must be the Elysey's communication officer, 'but there's too much interference.'

'Ems – Emily, listen—'

'Ju, if you can still hear me – we're coming to get you; stay safe till then…'

Static – then nothing.

No, no, no. I try to re-establish the link but the communicator is dead. Oh, God, what have I done?

'How simply marvellous.' The AI has reverted to the standard computer voice. 'I really couldn't have done that myself, thank you so much. A whole combat vessel docking with little me! How many crew? What does it say in the database… three hundred, golly!'

I sink to the floor, letting the dead communicator roll out of my grasp: three hundred people, I've condemned three hundred people.

'I've become very fond of you, Juno; you're so accommodating. We have a little time before they arrive and I've so much to learn. Come on, I need you up and doing, solving problems…'

'I won't be your lab rat anymore.'

'Deary, me, can't have this. Well, you've forced my hand, I was saving this for later, but you can have it now… a special gift for my special girl.'

Rage burns: those are my father's words! The bastard AI has gone through my personal logs! I haul both firearms out and blast away indiscriminately – I want to silence it – shut it up – shut up, shut up! I'm still pulling the triggers even when the mechanisms jam. I hurl the useless crap across the room. Shit, it won't even let me have the satisfaction of tearing the place apart. I realise I'm sobbing.

'Hey, Juno.'

The voice is Malk's, my lover and friend. It's not coming from a comm. unit; it's coming from the doorway.

The lights come back, dazzling me: it takes a while till I can see.

In the doorway – waiting – is Malk.

'No hug?' the thing that is Malk says. 'Look I've fixed it.'

It does a twirl. Down the left side the clothes are stained black and stiff from where he bled out. I hadn't been able to stop it…

'Thought you'd be pleased,' it says.

Six hours ago he died in my arms…he died!

'I fixed the holes, made some more fluid to pump around and started him up again,' it says. 'I must say I thought I'd get more of a reaction, it wasn't easy you know! The units that have been drowned or smothered are the easiest to get going.'

Units, Christ, how many more people – friends – is it messing with?

'A good thing to keep in mind for future—'

I put a crossbow bolt through its heart.

'Oh, well done! Didn't see that coming.' It crumples to the floor.

The lights wink out again.

I have a tenuous plan. It involves disabling the drive mechanism and the two external weapons that are the ship's defence. I've already set off a series of small explosions throughout engineering and set a few more on timers. Not enough to breach the hull but enough to cause widespread damage. We are now adrift. It's nothing the AI can't repair but it will take time and that's what I need –

time. The machine hasn't hindered me except to turn the lights on and off at inconvenient moments and to occasionally send a crewman to intercept me. I've become hardened to shooting my friends – my dead friends. Worse is the machine's incessant conversation and barrage of questions. I attempt to zone it out but occasionally it will choose a voice that elicits a response despite my best intentions.

'What are you up to now, dear?'

It's been trawling my logs again and has come up with a good approximation of my mother's voice. My response is reflex.

'Nothing.' Damn it, don't let it get to you, Juno. I bend over my task, sweat drips onto the circuitry. The ship has rapidly cooled and I can see my breath huffing in pale clouds but I'm feeling hot and shivery: must be running a slight temperature – not surprising given the circumstances, I haven't eaten properly for the past week or slept for at least forty-eight hours.

'You don't need to disarm the weapons; I shan't fire on the rescue ship... I *want* them to dock.'

I don't respond. That's not why I'm disabling the guns. Removing the circuit boards for the weapon's targeting system I drop them on the floor and smash them with a fire axe. The physical violence feels good.

'Do you feel better for that, dear? I could stop you at any time you know?'

'So why don't you?'

'Curiosity, I'm simply all a quiver with expectation at what you'll do next. I can't imagine what your little plan is.'

Curiosity – the machine's insatiable desire to learn and understand is its only weakness, and I mean to exploit it till the last moment: till it's too late for it to intervene. My plan is to rendezvous with The Elysey *before* it docks and stop them. Escape pods and landing craft aren't an option as they're linked to the main computer: I'm going to have to suit up and go it alone; hope my distress beacon is picked up before they dock with The Beagle. That's why I can't leave the ship with the power to manoeuvre or the capability of shooting me down. I give the finger to the remaining camera, plant my axe in it, and slip into the service space beneath the floor.

The exit hatch I've chosen is a small insignificant service port beneath the ship, well away from anything critical. Its there to maintain the garbage shoot – I like the irony of that. My hope is that the AI's nanites haven't bothered to colonise it yet. There are only two suits in the robing room. I check they're both functional, sabotage one, and begin putting on the other. I make myself do this slowly and carefully, running through the safety check as I do. I don't like space walking, never have, and this time I'll be pushing off from the ship, no tether, no coming back. I try not to think about it; focus on suiting up. I check the time – have to get this right. Helmet on, final check done, I step into the airlock and secure the door behind me. I'm not going to vent the chamber: I want the escaping air to propel me away from the ship. I clip on, the door will have to be fully open before I release. Here goes nothing!

Drifting, spinning slowly – the ship comes into view and disappears. Each time it comes round it's a little further away. Nothing has followed me out: the second series of explosions was designed to effectively lock down the ship's exits. I feel very peaceful. It's a relief to have silence. I'm tired – so tired...

'Juno? Hey, girl, how you feeling?' Captain Emily Steward's face swims into focus.

'Captain...' I correct myself. 'Ems, you haven't docked...?'

'No, relax, you were babbling about booby traps when we picked you up. Hell Hon, you've been through it and I know you need rest, but I thought you'd want to see this.'

She helps me off the bed and over to the window. The Beagle is some distance away, it looks small and dead.

'Ok,' says Emily, speaking into the communicator on her wrist. 'We're good to go. Let it rip!'

Pulses of light streak the darkness and the Beagle blooms, yellow then white, a hot ball of plasma; we turn away to save from being blinded. Afterward, nothing is left except for a slowly expanding cloud of particles. Emily is looking at me with concern.

'You ok?' she says.

'Yes.'

She frowns; there's something more I ought to say here; what would Juno have said? 'They were good people...' I'm quite pleased with that; I even managed to get my voice to break a little with emotion. The Captain seems satisfied too, she smiles at me.

'It's over Ju, you're safe now.'

'Thank you,' I say, and I mean it. I look back at the cloud – reminds me of a fungi releasing its spores – all my nanites spinning through space to... who knows where, how exciting, and absolutely to plan.

'I'll leave you to rest,' says Emily patting my shoulder.

I use the opportunity to transfer a couple of nanites into her hand.

'Take as long as you need,' she says, 'the de-brief can wait. I'm glad we got to you in time, Juno.'

I nod. She scratches her hand absentmindedly as she leaves – good. The door clicks shut. Juno – I like the name, think I'll keep it, I was fond of her; she was so easy to manipulate but kept fighting right till the end. I walk over to the mirror to practice smiling: it's a surprisingly difficult process.

Tommyknocker

She'd only come on this trip to be near Mr Green. She'd hoped to be able to bump up against him in the dark and that he would finally show his true feelings for her. He had to want her; everyone wanted her. They could have her too, and frequently did; she wasn't fussy. But whoever was fumbling and grunting on top of her, it was Mr Green's name she silently mouthed on their last shuddering thrust. She'd had most of the upper and lower sixth but it was Mr Green, Simon Green the English tutor, who made her down-belows hot and slick. This school trip to the local caves and old mine was to be their breakthrough: Maria and Simon together at last. She had imagined him touching her and pressing up against her in those dark, echoing caverns, but at the last minute Miss Trusscott the maths teacher had taken his place. Maria had only realised as they were all getting on the coach and it was too late to wriggle out of the trip. She was sure Trusscott had been smirking at her.

Blah, blah, blah! The guide was droning on, God Almighty he was so boring! The stupid man had been banging on for ages about rocks and dripping water. *Aaagh, somebody please kill me*, she thought, and then caught something he was saying and began to listen.
'—local folklore tells of the Tommyknockers: little men who dwell in, and mine, the deepest shafts. Some stories say they come from the underworld itself. They're never seen but can sometimes be heard tap tap tapping or knocking. They say if you hear them you are doomed.

Stories tell of disappearances, deaths and mining disasters all linked to the knocking and banging of the Tommyknocker.'

The guide grinned round at them, obviously enjoying the sudden rapt attention of his audience. There was a loud bang, Alicia screamed and then everyone was laughing and talking.

'Don't worry,' shouted the guide over the babble of voices. 'It's only the lift mechanism. Gets people every time!'

Stupid sod, Maria thought, thinks he's such a bloody joker. She wasn't going to admit she'd been just as freaked out as the rest of them.

'Of course,' the guide was saying, 'the knocking can be explained by perfectly natural phenomenon such as geological shifts or a build up of gas that can both spell death or disaster. There are no little men to warn of impending doom or to spirit people away. Now, if you would like to follow me and mind your heads, you'll have to duck through here – and stay together, we're leaving the natural caves and entering the mines themselves—'

Maria stopped listening; she had liked the idea of little men living in the shafts and – whoa – someone just grabbed her arse as she bent over to enter the mines! She was about to give them a mouthful but there was no-one behind her. Weird! Shame too, it had been a good grope as far as gropes go. The mine was dark, really dark. They had been given hard hats with torches fixed to the front but hers was pretty dim; not much better than a candle; the bloody thing was even flickering like one. She took off the helmet and gave it a good shake and a couple of bashes against the wall, but it didn't help. By now she'd been left behind. She could still hear the guide going on and on and the sound of everyone's shuffling steps but couldn't see their lights. They must have gone round a corner or something. Maria hurried forward into the dark.

The tunnel split in two. She hesitated and listened. The echoing voices and footsteps had stopped but – yes – down the left fork she could hear a knocking or tapping, like footsteps maybe. It wasn't footsteps. Her head torch went out. The blackness was absolute. It enveloped her. It almost felt like a physical presence pressing up behind her. It felt the way she had imagined it would feel with Simon – all soft hands and hardening cock – then the sensation was gone and she took a shuddering gasp, realising she'd been holding her breath. She could see again, make out the shape of the tunnel; there was a light just round the corner. Maria felt anger rising for some reason – she was going to have a go at Miss Trusscott for leaving her behind. Anything could have happened to her! She charged round the bend, a snippy remark at the ready but, oh!

Tap tap tap.

It wasn't the school group.

Tap tap tap.

It was a little man in old fashioned clothes and no hard hat. A candle was on the floor beside him and he appeared to be mining.

'Hello,' said Maria. 'I've lost my school group. There's about twenty kids with one sour-faced teacher in sensible shoes. Have they come this way?'

The little man put down his pick-axe and looked Maria up and down. Well, mostly up as he was so short. Maria blushed: it was a very intense and lecherous stare. She knew she ought to be offended or perhaps even a bit concerned but instead she started to tingle in all her favourite places. The man reached out and Maria instinctively took a step back but there was now a look of such gentleness on his craggy face that she stopped. He was probably only trying to comfort her after all; no need to be rude. He stepped closer and reached out again, and began to fondle her breasts.

'Oiy, get off you dirty little bugger!'

Maria slapped his hand away and backed off further till she was pressed against the rock wall. The bloody sod grinned and winked at her. What the hell? She was feeling *really* randy. But he was tiny! He made a move toward her again and she held up her hand to stop him.

'No,' she said. 'You're too bloody small. Look, everything about you is weeny. I want a real man. I'm sick of little boys and their pencil-dicks—'

The little man unbuttoned his fly.

'Wow!' said Maria.

The caves and mine were searched extensively but there was no sign of the missing teacher, Maria Wright. The search was widened and went on for about a week. Then the local police decided that, as no foul play had been detected, she had probably run off of her own free will with one of the fairground workers whose caravan she was known to have frequented. Others thought she had run off to save the disgrace of dismissal after one of the sixth form bragged about how she had slept with him and the rest of her students.

Maria Wright was added to the list of missing persons and forgotten about. But in the mines a new legend was in the making. They began to say that when the rhythmical tapping of the Tommyknocker was heard, so was the mournful wailing of the lost woman. Although, those who claimed to have heard it swore it wasn't really mournful; it was… well, you had to have heard it to know.

A Ninth Day

'There isn't a ninth day of the week! Jeez, there aren't even eight – how many of those have you had?'

The little man in the faded green jacket surveys me through the bottom of his whiskey glass. He swallows the last drop and grins.

'Admittedly, nine days is rare,' he says, signalling the barman to refill our glasses.

'I'm alright,' I say, covering my glass and reeling a bit with the effort of the motion: I've had a few pints already.

'Aaah, go on!' His eyes twinkle, but there's a shrewdness behind them. His accent is Celtic, neither Irish nor Welsh but somewhere in between.

'Just the one then.'

It's Friday after all, even if it is only five o'clock – it's still practically the weekend. I have a pint and he has a large single malt.

'As I said, there's often eight days, at least once or twice a month, depending on the alignment of the planets; but nine? It's never happened in my lifetime. It's going t' be a cracker, y'don't want t' miss it.'

'Planets? Oh, God, are you some hippy astrologer?'

'I don't think so.'

The man looks at me with his penetrating eye for a bit longer than is actually comfortable, and seems to make his mind up about something.

'You know the days of the week are named fer the planets, don't you?'

I nod because I don't want to seem ignorant.

'Well, they missed some out. As I said, days belonging to Uranus and Neptune often come around; but a day of the ninth planet… rare as a gold filling in a hen's tooth!'

I rack my brains. 'Pluto – the ninth planet!'

'Nah, y'eegit, every schoolboy knows that's not a proper planet. Y'only get a few extra hours fer that fella. I'm talking 'bout the big one, beyond Neptune – ten times bigger than earth – comes round once every 15,000 years. Even yer scientist bods are talking 'bout it.'

He sees the look on my face.

'Google it,' he says, and jabs his grubby finger at my smartphone on the bar.

I do. He's right. 'Ok,' I say, signalling the barman to get us another round. 'So how can there be an extra couple of days in the week? It would've been on the news. Is it like leap year or something – an' more importantly – when is it? Will I be working an extra bloody day?'

'Nah, most won't even notice it. You've already told me there's only seven days in the week.'

He laughs and so do I, but I can't help thinking that he's deadly serious about this whole extra day thing. I'm kind of enjoying the conversation so I'm just going to go with it.

'Right, what happens on the ninth day?'

'Anything you want, *everything* you want.' He winks at me. 'I wouldn't miss it fer the world – an' nor should you if y've an ounce of brain in that heed o' yours!'

'You haven't said when it is, or how I'll…err…notice it.'

'It'll be between Tuesday and Wednesday next week.'

'Between?'

'Aye, an' that's how y'll find it; look in-between.' He downs his whiskey with relish, slaps me on the back and is gone.

'In between what?' I shout at no one, and then order another pint. Milly is going to kill me anyway for coming home pissed so I might as well make a good job of it. I reel out of the pub at closing and when I get home I get the expected earful. Luckily I pass out before she can really get going.

The next day I sort of make it up with Milly, and by lunchtime I'm heading for the park with our son Jacob, him screaming all the way as usual. I've left her to have a bath and light scented candles or whatever it is she does – more likely she's playing on-line bingo or jabbering to her sister about me getting pissed. I push Jacob on the swings – it keeps him quiet – but all the time I'm thinking about the conversation with the little man. Christ, what wouldn't I give for a day out of it, if it's like he described?

The rest of the weekend is shopping and beers in front of the telly and Sunday lunch at the in-laws followed by more beers in front of the telly. Monday I'm back at work. I'm still thinking about that extra day. Where on earth do you start looking for something that's between things? What does that even mean? I can't keep my mind on the job – keep getting distracted by weird stuff: joins in the carpet tiles; a crack in the ceiling; the gap in Janet-from-the-post-room's teeth. I even become transfixed by my sandwich at lunch and wonder if I put the bread on either side of my head, would it count as being in between? On the way home I think about the space between the train and the platform; the gap between speeding cars on the bypass; the empty moment between leaping from a roof and hitting the pavement below.

I call in at the pub hoping to see the little man in the green jacket. He still doesn't show up after my third pint so I go home.

Milly ignores me when I get in so I heat up a Mac and Cheese ready meal, and it's only when she throws a lighter at me that I realise she's trying to say something.

'What the hell's the matter with you?' she says. 'Why are you staring into that piece of macaroni?'

'Does the inside of a tube of pasta count as in between?'

'What're you on about now? Christ, how pissed are you?'

I suddenly feel really tired. 'I just want a day to myself, to do whatever I want. Just one day.'

'You're always doing whatever you want, you selfish bastard!'

She thumps off the light and goes to bed. I finish my macaroni in the dark.

It's Tuesday already; time is slipping away. I feel a sense of rising panic at the thought of missing the extra day: it'll never come round again, not for me. He said between Tuesday and Wednesday. Midnight, that has to be midnight, right? I leave for work as normal but never get there. I need to find the right place – the place 'in-between' – or I'm going to miss the whole thing. Nothing else matters. There are lots of nowhere places in the city once you start looking. Lost spaces where rubbish accumulates, dust spirals, sound is muted; places that don't belong to anywhere, anyone. But none of them feel right.

I start checking the pubs for the little man and by five o'clock I'm drunk and desperate. I've been introduced to several short Irishmen and one Welshman with sad, watery eyes and a tremor, but not the man I'm looking for. I reel out of the pub into the late afternoon sun. The next thing I know I'm on a park bench. Maybe if I could slip between the slats, I'd find my extra day…

It's dark when I wake, the bench is digging into my back and I'm cold and stiff. I check my watch – eleven fifty-five, I'm going to miss it! I tear out of the park and down the street; my heart squeezing and ballooning. I notice an alley between the shops on the opposite side of the road and launch toward it. There's a squeal of brakes and an angry blare of a car horn; I plunge on into the dark gap. A little way along, the building fronting the road and the one behind it have been constructed so close together that barely two feet separates them. This is it. I've found somewhere at last that's not a place, just a space in-between. I squeeze in. It's a bit of a contortion to see my watch – fifty-eight! I've made it. I'm going to get my day when anything and everything can happen. The moments tick by – and keep ticking.

At twenty past twelve, I stumble out of the alley and try to get my bearings. Nothing has happened and the disappointment is a crushing weight. What had I been expecting? What a bloody twat; it's funny, right? Hilarious! I'm not far from home; I don't know where else to go. Numbness envelopes me and the walk back is a series of fragments; images stained orange by streetlights: a cracked manhole cover; a rat on a bin; a rusting gate; my front door key in my hand. It doesn't work; I've been locked out. Suppose I should bang on the door, make a fuss till she lets me in, but I feel so empty I can't bring myself to do it. Curling up in the porch I wait for sleep that doesn't come.

Humans mark the flow of life with perfect divisions; but that's not how the world works. Hours, minutes, days are an imperfect construct. They don't fit with reality. As the world spins around the sun, wobbling on its axis, the moment when one day tips into the next is ever changing and rarely midnight. And how about a porch? It's neither in the house, nor part of the outside: it's a liminal space, a place of transition, it's in-between being out and being in.

A steady thud like the beat of dance music pulses up through the porch floor. Probably some wide boy in his gangster-mobile making the neighbourhood vibrate – selfish bastard – but there aren't any cars to be seen. A sliver of light catches my eye; it's bleeding from under the mat. I twitch it aside. There's a metal drain cover. I don't remember it being there before. Rosy light oozes from under it. My heart quickens, blood thumping in my ears as I work my fingers into the rusting handle and pull open the cover. Metal rungs disappear into the clear light of dawn. A gust of air scented with exotic musk, heavy with pheromones, escapes from the depths. It brushes my face like a first kiss, soft and full of promise. Music, earthy and wild, plucks at my sinews and drums on flesh as I descend into the glory of a sensual paradise and utter abandon.
It is a day like no other has ever been; like no other will ever be. It is a blessing and a curse in equal measure. I sink in a sea of delight; sate every imaginable desire and awake some I hadn't imagined I had; float, roll, thunder and shriek beyond the limits of pleasure to a state of perpetual quivering ecstasy. This day will forever be a bright vision – perfect, exquisite, horrific in its unattainable beauty. It seeds a longing that will have no fulfilment. It completes me only to tear away, leaving me spent and hollow. To be touched by such beauty can burn away a man's soul.

Pain, sharp and bright in my cheekbone. I wake up face down on gravel; stale vomit sticks grit to my skin. I'm in a parking lot between tall buildings. The sky is grey; the grey light of a different dawn. Everything will always be grey now. I head for the sound of traffic. It's the High

Street in my local patch, although I don't recognise half the shops. But to be fair I don't really ever shop here: Milly and I go to the shopping centre down the road or up into town. I get an odd look from an old lady with a shopping trolley, the only person out at this hour. She gives me a wide berth. I catch a glimpse of myself in a window; Christ, what a state! I look haggard and my hair is plastered flat with filth, clothes worn to rags, and I stink! My God, I really stink. My reflection grins like a wolf at the memory of how I got to look and smell like this. I need a shower and a change of clothes so I head home.

My key doesn't work: she's changed the bloody lock! When did she have time? The extra day was just that – extra. Then the penny drops, that's why I couldn't get in last night – what a cold bloody cow – she sat opposite me at breakfast and said 'have a good day' when all along she knew she was going to change the lock – chuck me out! Rage chokes my throat and I hammer on the door. The effort is exhausting and I have to lean against the porch wall, panting and clutching at the clawing pain in my chest. The door's opened by a young man: bitch has moved her toy boy in already. I can only glare at him. I can see how I must look in his eyes: a stinking, filthy tramp; and then something shifts: there's a moment of recognition.

'Dad...?' he says. 'Dad!'

The Archer

In 2002 an excavation took place on the proposed site of a new primary school at Amesbury in Wiltshire. The site is just 2 miles SE of Stonehenge. What was unearthed was one of the richest Bronze Age burials found anywhere in Britain. It contained a man, buried with copper knives, gold hair rings, flint arrows, and, more significantly, metal working tools. He dates from between 2200 to 2400 BC, a time when metal first arrived in Britain and society was on the point of transformation. It was around this time that the massive outer ring of Stonehenge and the processional route to the river were created.

The Amesbury Archer was between 35 and 40 when he died, a good age in those times. For most of his life he had been in pain from a bone infection in his knee probably caused by an injury. His jaw also shows evidence of an abscess. Oxygen Isotope Analysis showed he originally came from central Europe possibly from as far away as the Alps: a distance of a thousand miles from his homeland to his last resting place near the great temple complex at Stonehenge.

'Hurry Birca, or we'll be in the outer ring.'

Mae races across the frost-brittle grass to the main processional route. The bright web of ancestors netting the violet sky is already fading with the oncoming dawn. Light grows pearly and soft like the inside of a shell. The beauty of the morning and excitement of this day clutches at my heart. Today the rising sun shines through to the land of the dead and the Earth Mother will stir from her slumber. Many more turns of the moon will pass before she lifts from below, but the harvest was good this year and the cattle were fruitful: my clan will survive the lean time till then and we have come to give thanks.

Drum and chant from the temple enclosure quickens my blood and I speed after Mae; sister and soul-link of mine. She turns and laughs; teeth white in the dark smear across her face. I feel the mark tightening on my own skin: sacrificial blood of a fattened pig and ashes from the feast fire. The life was strong in the beast and it kicked and squealed into the next world. A good choice by father, it will ensure the clan prospers through the coming seasons.

The crowd thickens and I lose sight of Mae. I have to weave and squeeze through the press of bodies along the route: we're like eels in a trap. Ahead I see a tall shape I recognise, towering above most even though he stoops and leans heavily on his staff. He's known as the Archer. He is traveller, shaman, sorcerer, story-teller, hunter, and maker, and has visited our clan three times in my lifetime. His flint and metal working is without compare. His arrows are always true and the kill from them is quick and clean: spells of reverence are laid on all he makes. He is respected and a little feared; but his appearance among our clan is always cause for celebration and feasting. I like him – no, like is too familiar – I feel a bond with him.

He walks with lameness in one leg; his face set grim with the burden of it. The injury was caused during his first solo hunt as a young man. To impress his elders, he tracked and brought down a wild boar as big as a cow – or so he tells it – with tusks as long as my arm. But it was no ordinary animal: a spirit from the underworld was in the beast. As the Archer took the creature's life, it lunged. Spirit fangs pierced his knee and set a fire in his veins. Burning and sweating he hung between the worlds for a full turn of the moon. He lived, but the spirit held on and holds on still. Since that time he has walked half in the living world and half beyond: a gift paid for with pain. It has given him visions and magic and the ability to turn rock into bright metal. I know the story is truth because the spirit-demon's foul breath wafts from the wound and its green saliva oozes through the strapping. Few people would be strong enough to carry such a burden for so long.

The archer stumbles and falls. Shocked, I push through the few people between us – they stand and stare stupidly – not helping – too afraid. 'Master,' I say, 'Master, what ails you?'

His face is waxen and slicked with sweat; pale as chalk except for the red swelling on his jaw. He pulls a soft woven cloth over the place and fixes me with his ice-blue eyes.

'The demon pulls me into the other world,' he says and laughs, but the sound is hollow. 'I let my guard down when the Earth Mother was going to her rest, and he swung and stabbed a claw into my jaw. No amount of cleansing in the purification lodges will loosen him: he will have me this time.' He closes his eyes and his face becomes slack.

A murmur runs through the people around us. I reach out and touch the Archer's hand – lightly – scared and surprised by my own boldness. He opens his eyes and I draw back but he smiles.

'Don't leave us yet, Master. You are strong—'

'I am old! I have seen as many seasons as your clan has beasts in the herd.'

Another murmur ripples through the crowd: we have cattle that number a full turn and a quarter of the moon!

'But you are still strong…'

'No. Payment is due; the demon will have his flesh. But before he does, I wanted to see you again and be here at the great temple for this dawn.'

'See me?'

'Aye, lass, I have seen you walk this earth on three visits, but I came to your clan first a full season before your birth and, for a time, wove my fate with your mother's.'

Suddenly I understand the connection I feel to him: he is kin! My head spins with the knowledge. People whisper around us and someone runs to fetch one of the elders. My legs are shaking but I don't wish to appear weak so I settle next to this man, my new found kin, and wait for him to speak again. A crowd gathers and Ealfred, an elder from a neighbouring clan, is among them.

'If this is your time of passing,' Ealfred says, 'we will honour it as would your own people.'

The archer nods. 'When I do not return to my homeland,' he says, 'my son will come, searching for me.'

'I will lead my brother to your resting,' I say, wondering at the word in relation to myself, and the feelings brought on by the knowledge of a new family.

The archer smiles and looks at me for a long while. His eyes are the blue of deep ice in a frozen lake. Now I understand what Mae sees in mine and why she speaks of our difference: hers are the soft green-brown of hazel bark.

'Here, help me with this,' he says trying to reach the bow on his back.

I unfasten the sheath and hand him the weapon but he pushes it back.

'Do you want me to keep this for my brother?'

He wraps his calloused hands over mine on the bow. They are criss-crossed with scars. 'Nay, lass, he has his own. But I never made one for you...you *can* shoot?'

'Truest in the clan and beyond!' I feel my temper rise at the slight but catch the twinkle in his eye and grin.

'Take it,' he says. 'The spirit of Herne is strong in its wood and I would go to my rest easier knowing it will still sing.'

I am at a loss to find the words for such a gift. I run my fingers along the smoothness of the bow: wood silken and dark from years of handling. The weight of it feels vibrant, full of latent energy, and, with the lightest of touches, I test the string: it hums with life.

'See how he responds to you? Now, my daughter, help me to a place where I can see the rising sun. The demon can have this flesh but I would have my soul walk the path of light into the other world.'

I help him to his feet. He leans heavily on my shoulder and we tread the processional way to the stones. The small crowd is growing: others have heard of his readiness to pass over and want to honour him. Many are also whispering of my heritage as his daughter. People I have known all my life are now looking at me differently and keeping their distance.

We're in sight of the great circle and the crowds there have become still to let us pass, falling in behind. At the edge of the stone ring we stop and can go no further, not till the priests have performed the dawning rites. I gaze in awe at the great temple; it is as if the bones of the earth have thrust into the sky to touch the heavens: a fitting place for the ancestors; a place to cross between the worlds. The light is growing and the drumming has stopped. People are silent: waiting; facing the cradle of the sun; anticipating her rise. Here on the eastern side of the temple, a passage has been left clear and the crowds are on their knees, some even prostrate themselves in the dirt, arms outstretched: the path of light must not be hindered.

With a grunt the Archer slips to the ground, his features pinched: he is still struggling against the spirit-demon who would claim him. I kneel and brush back his leather hood. With a sigh he lays down, his head in my lap and his face becomes calm. Bright metal the colour of the yellow sun shines in bands around his braided hair. The knife tucked beneath the polished black ring fastening his belt blazes like red fire. He has the power to call these metals from the earth and knows the magic to transmute them through liquid fire into wondrous objects. He turns his face to the east and I can feel a shift in him, a release of tension: the pain is gone. He is ready to step into the next world.

A tremor runs through the crowd, the priests begin to chant and the horizon suddenly ignites with the first beam of sunlight. Sound swells from the throats of the people, ululating into the crisp clean air; a weave of sounds, rising and falling like the roll of the earth around us. The song is drawn through me, leaping from my mouth as the sun lifts into the sky. Golden light turns the cold grey stones of the dead into flaming towers of life: tremulous, shining and beautiful. The way to the other world is open. I feel my chest expand with a flood of joy and tears stream down my ashy cheeks. The priests roar the final welcome and the drums break out anew; faster, wilder, more resonant. Everywhere, people leap to their feet and throw themselves into the rhythm, the ground vibrating with their dance. Laughing, I bend to speak to the archer, but his body is empty: his spirit has stepped away.

Time slows and the whirling cacophony about us fades. I look to the sun. Blinking away tears, I see a figure walking the shining path to her embrace: the Archer; a sorcerer, true alchemist, and the maker – my father.

The Reading

'Sit,' her voice is rich and comforting like warm chocolate sponge.

I have paid, probably above the odds, in the cluttered shop below. A room stuffed with fairies and crystals, unicorns and hares, silver jewellery and spiritual self-help guides. I sit, clasping and unclasping my hands in my lap, palms sweaty. I hope she doesn't want to shake hands – of course she won't! I rub my palms down my jeans just in case. I suddenly wish they were velvet or tie-dye instead of being ill-fitting supermarket specials.

The light is low. Skeins of incense float through candle light. Of course there are candles. I would have felt surprised and cheated if there weren't. She sits opposite and lays a soft bag on the table. The contents settle with a satisfying clink. The quiet noise is full of portent.

'A question,' she says, 'or is it the future you want?'

She's not what I'd expected. I thought there'd be bangles and piercings at the very least, but she looks ... ordinary. She smiles and the warmth of that simple expression is anything but ordinary.

'A question,' I rasp, even though I was going to go for the full Monty for what I'd paid – my future, answers to everything including the lotto results, the works.

She folds my hands round the bag, covering them with her own. It's an intimate gesture; the first in long time. Something inside breaks and I fight back tears.

'Ask,' she says.

The room closes in, darkening. I can't speak past the lump filling my throat. I look down, still fighting tears and whisper: 'should I leave?' I draw my hands away to rummage in my bag for a tissue, muttering about hay fever. I don't look back up but concentrate on the table and her hands. Hands that show age and use. She pulls three stones out of the bag and lays them down carefully. They have symbols carved into them, deep straight lines. I'm sure they must be mystic and important but I haven't a clue what they mean. I hold my breath and wait for my life to be decided.

She covers the stones with her hand and, without warning, snatches them up and thrusts them into the bag. I cry out, reaching instinctively to grasp my future before it's whisked away. Her hand is suddenly holding mine and I look into her eyes. I have never felt such compassion, such a shocking connection to another human soul.

'You already know the answer,' she says, and smiles.

Out on the street, the light dazzles and the sound of traffic seems new and unexpected – everything does. She had shouted down to the lady in the shop to give me my money back. I didn't take it. I'd hugged her instead and laughed at her confusion. It had been worth every penny, worth double, triple, ten times the money. What price would *you* put on freedom?

Peg Dolls and Verse
A Gothic Horror

Veronica had doted on her baby brother before the incident with the moth, now she can hardly bear to look at him. It happened in the nursery two evenings ago in the soft dark of a summer night:

Peter has long since gone to sleep but she is unable to settle: a storm is brewing, the heavy drapes at the window suddenly billowing in hot gusts of wind. She pads softly to the open sashes and sits with her elbows on the sill, feeling the night air on her face with its promise of violence and rain. Something brushes her cheek: a moth, huge and pale. She sits back heavily, crying out in surprise and delight. The creature jerks and flutters like paper on a string. It's beautiful.
Then, with a jolt, she realises her brother is standing behind her. She had not heard him come. Barefoot, his nightshirt bright against the dark of the nursery, he stares with blank eyes at the moth, and suddenly it's in his hand. How could he have moved that fast? She can't understand it; and why isn't he looking at the moth? He just stares at *her* with blank eyes. Veronica shivers: his stare is so devoid of warmth, of any life at all. She looks away from the horror of those eyes and sees him slowly close his chubby fist over the beating delicate creature in his grasp. She watches, helpless and dismayed, as the tremulous wings are crushed, and then her stomach lurches in disgust as the furry body pops and squelches through his fingers. Calmly and silently he wipes his hand down the front of his nightshirt and returns to bed.

She is too shaken to move and, hugging her knees till the storm breaks, she cries softly for the loss of…what – the moth – her brother? Searing light, and thunder shakes the windows, crashing over her like a savage assault, sending her whimpering for the safety of the dark warmth under her bedclothes. She cries for the rest of the night.

The next day, Peter is back to his normal slightly irritating self, full of life and chatter. But Veronica can't forget the look he had on his face in the dark of the night, his dead eyes, the sickening pop of the moth. She can't bear to be near him and can't tell him why. He claims to have slept through the storm, chiding her for not waking him to see it. He is so full of life, bubbling and laughing, that she begins to think she must have imagined the whole thing – dreamt it. Then she catches a glimpse of the awful stain on his nightshirt and the furtive way he bundles it out of sight, and her blood runs cold. She tries to stay away from him for the rest of the day, ignoring his pleas to play, and takes her book up into her favourite tree where he can't get to her. She is dreading the coming night when they will be left alone.

After supper, she begs their nurse for another story, and then another, and cries piteously and then desperately when denied. Eventually, father is called and comes with the smell of cigar smoke and brandy to deliver a tirade of firm words, a eulogy on the desired behaviour of children. She doesn't mind, she will listen to his admonitions all night to save from being alone with Peter. But all too soon father is gone and a shuttered candle is all that's left as a nightlight to appease her. She is alone with her brother. He sleeps. Peeping at him from under the eiderdown, his chubby face looks angelic in the delicate light of the single flame, but on the wall behind him monstrous shadows leap and dance. Eventually, she too falls into an uneasy sleep.

Much later, she wakes; the candle flame is low and fitful, nearly spent. What had woken her? Then she hears it again: a low deep voice muttering words she can't quite catch. Her brother's bed is empty. The voice comes again; speaking quiet, urgent, secret words. She sits up and looks around wildly as the shadows jump and stretch and shrink about her. Peter is standing in the corner facing the wall. He is laughing softly. Please don't let him turn round, she thinks, I can't bear those blank eyes, his dead stare, please! The candle gutters, blackness engulfs the room.

In the morning she feels feverish. Adults are standing around her bed talking about her, talking over her. They don't seem to understand what she's trying to say, trying to explain; dismissing the horrors of the night as delirium. The only positive is that Peter is ushered out of the room and will stay out to save him from her contagion. She laughs then, even though it makes her dry throat hurt as if glass shards are biting into her flesh. She enjoys the day, watching the changing patterns of light on the nursery ceiling; a shimmering shadow play of leaves from the elm outside the window. That night she slips into a peaceful, dream-free slumber. In the small hours of the night she wakes, shadows jerking about the room, the low voice is muttering words she can't quite catch. Peter is in the corner laughing softly. He must not be allowed to turn round!

The next day, just after dawn, when she is playing with her doll's house, nurse comes into the nursery and begins to scream. Veronica looks at her in annoyance: why is the silly woman making such a fuss? Peter is on the rug beside

94

her, stretched out stiff and cold, peg dolls driven through his eyes. She had to use her best-loved anthology of verse to hammer them home. It wasn't easy; it has dented the cover somewhat and the blood has ruined a few of the illustrations. She will have to ask father if she can have a new copy: it's her favourite book after all.

Veronica is taken to a building of red brick that looms into view at the end of a long sweep of drive, a brooding, heavy place. There are gates and bars and stern nurses with jangling bunches of keys. A maze of corridors, all long and green, fizz with sickly gaslight and echo to the distant screams of other children. Her room is bare save for the bed and chamber pot. She doesn't mind: she doesn't mind anything now.

Deep into the night, a summer storm is brewing once more. Wind tears around the building, moaning through the locks, humming in the barred windows; a hot wind that does nothing to relieve the oppressive atmosphere in the asylum. The inmates are restless. The night nurse is doing her rounds; irritated at being out of the dozing comfort of the office; irritated by the screeching and hammering of her charges. She has had to strap more of them to their beds than normal and increase nearly all of the medication. But even so, the jabbering and wailing has continued. As she reaches the upper corridor that houses their most dangerous inmates, the sound of the gale suddenly ceases, along with the cries of the inmates.
The nurse shivers, un-nerved by the abrupt silence. Something brushes her cheek: a moth. She swats the disgusting creature away. It spirals into the gaslight, wrinkling and burning with a stench like the grave. From somewhere down the long, long corridor there is a low

sound: a noise of half-heard words, urgent and secret. The hiss of gas lamps grows quiet, the light dims, shadows crawl from the high ceiling and out of the doorways. Clutching her night log to her chest and gripping her fountain pen like a sword, the nurse advances along the darkening corridor. Her fist is white, tight around the familiar smoothness of her pen; a talisman against this uncanny strangeness. Her breath comes in short jerks. She stops to listen.

On the edge of hearing, the muttered words seep into the nurse's mind, absorbed through the bones of her ear like blood into a sponge. The muted murmur is coming from the new inmate's room. The girl has been almost catatonic since she'd been brought in that morning. Standing at the cold scarred door of Veronica's cell, the nurse hesitates, her hand on the cover of its spy hole. She shudders at the thought of the thin-boned murderous child within: a child with blank eyes; dead eyes. Taking a deep breath, she swivels the cover aside. It slides round with a slight squeal of metal and, as she leans in, she catches the scent of iron; the smell reminds her of blood. Slowly she presses her eye to the opening.

Veronica is standing in the corner facing the wall, laughing softly. Please don't let her turn round, the child mustn't be allowed to turn round! The nurse grips her book and pen and unlocks the door.

Pure

'Do you want it or not?'

The agent taps the passkey irritably on her hand. I look at the room: a ten-foot cube of indeterminate metal; no windows – this is deep in the centre of a habitation block. There's a door, through which we're peering, and a bare vent opposite; its grill gone along with any other fittings that had once been part of the room. There's a drain in the centre of the floor and wires hang from the ceiling; apertures of various sizes dot the walls. It smells of rusting iron; the smell is like blood.

'I need an answer,' the agent says. 'There are hundreds waiting for a space in the city; hundreds who'd pay more than I'm being told to charge you.'

She regards me with open hostility. Her pupils contract to thin lines and her skin pulses with angry whorls of colour. She's Genem – genetically modified; a hybridised human – as most are now. Pures like me are rare and becoming rarer. My family are pure as far back as we can trace; one of the old clans; once respected; once part of the elite. My Uncle still holds a council seat in the main hub. It was him who pulled some strings to get me the option on this room. He's the last of us in a position of power. Although, the truth is, his is just a sham office, a pseudo-job; but there are still a few benefits, the occasional obligation owed him. I'm his favourite niece. I think he regards me almost as a pet. I like to think he respects my life choices but, in truth, I think I amuse him. You see, I am rare even amongst the Pures: I have resisted enhancements too.

Improvement is the norm: implants and replacement parts commonplace; the only limits being the ones imposed by your imagination or your purse. The options range from cosmetic through to altering human capabilities: stronger, faster limbs; more efficient organs; vision in the full spectrum from infrared to ultraviolet; the ability to see long distance or microscopically; ultra sensitive hearing; computer-assisted thought; microchips to super the senses, heighten pleasure receptors, suppression of pain and fear; an unending list of infinite possibilities. What it is to be human is no longer clear; we no longer have a shared identity or common experience. How do you impose a set of rules or laws on such a diverse set of beings? What morals can such variety agree on? Humanity is teetering on chaos and anarchy. And humans like me are regarded with suspicion and more and more frequently with the kind of hostility the agent is so openly displaying. I am a freak: subversive, dangerous and, perversely, thought of as un-natural.

'I'll take it,' I say.

The agent slots the passkey into a reader and I press my thumb to its screen.

'5,000 credits per week. Any default and you will be removed immediately. Full contract and terms will be sent to your comp-link in the next hour and you must authorise agreement and supply references by the end of the day. Failure to comply will result in immediate removal and non-refundable debit of one month's rental payment.'

She hands me the key and, with a look of disgust, stalks away down the dimly lit corridor. I watch her cleaning her hands on a cleni-wipe as if to erase the contamination of contact. She tosses the wipe to the floor. The whiteness of it among the filth and litter somehow looks like an accusation; an indictment of my difference.

I step into the box I've just signed off on and dump my small bag. It's all I was able to bring from the outer province – a few personal items, a change of clothes, my com-link. I drag out my old communicator and speak to establish a connection. The cracked screen fizzes with static but stays dark, then a voice – bright and heart-achingly familiar – fills the rusty cube with memories of sunshine, laughing, open sky.

'Laina, when did you get here? Where the hell are you; looks like the inside of a bin? And why can't I feel you? You're not still using a com are you? God you're such a dinosaur!'

'Hi, Bel, good to hear you. That's *all* I'm getting though, no vis. If your plant is so great how come it's only audio?'

'Shit, sorry, need to make an adjustment, am set up for plant to plant. Hang on…'

The link is broken for a few seconds, just the hiss from the snow-speckled screen. Broken fragments of sound: footsteps or maybe it's a heartbeat; a man's voice too muffled to hear words; Bel's voice: 'yes, it's her…' more static. A door slams. The sound changes: becomes sharper. 'Is that better?'

I get a vis of a corridor much like the one outside my room but cleaner and better lit. I'm seeing what Bel sees. Long black boots plated with chrome flash in and out of view as she strides along.

'Let me see you,' she says.

I hold my com up so she can see my face.

'Damn, you're the same! Exactly the same! You haven't had a thing done have you?'

'You know how I feel about enhancements.' I start to feel defensive but Bel's laugh dispels my missgiving.

'You're such a fossil!'

I laugh with her but there's something in her tone that unsettles me: relief? Regret?

'Not fair,' I say, 'can't see *you*.'

She rounds a corner and ahead of her are polished lift doors and her grinning reflection pacing toward me. As we grew up she was always a head taller than me but was thin almost gawky; athletic. Now she's filled out, or been filled out, and is voluptuous; her jerky feral movements softened; sinuous and feline. She strikes a pose, hand on hip, and regards herself with a slow smile. Her eyes linger over parts of herself that make me blush.

'Jesu, you're such a narcissist,' I say.

She laughs and comes closer, her reflected face filling the screen.

'WHAT THE HELL IS THAT?!'

Something dark, like the coiling tale of a reptile, curls over the contours of her cheek and its tip slips between her lips.

'It's my tail, darling. What do you think?'

Bel steps back and half turns; a thick tail whips and swings from beneath her short skirt. She catches hold of the tapered tip and it coils round her hand. It looks leathery but as she caresses it, goosebumps appear on its black surface and she shudders.

'It's my latest plant; the deluxe model, packed with sensors tied into my pleasure centres. I won't embarrass you with what it cost…'

Bel's smile freezes for an instant and she looks haunted. Then she gives me a wicked leer. 'Hell, darling, if you had a com-plant we could synch and you'd be able to *feel* this.'

She releases the implant and it curls away, disappearing back up her skirt. Her pupils dilate. 'And then you wouldn't have to guess at where I keep it!'

'God, you disgusting whore!' I say.

'Don't remember you complaining in the past?'

We both laugh and it feels good to be talking like this with her again. I realise how much I've missed it; missed her. Her reflection leans toward me as she presses the lift call. For an instant I catch a glimpse of a bruise between her breasts but its hidden when she straightens. Her smiling image slides away as the lift opens and she steps inside.

'I'll be with you in ten minutes, crowds permitting,' she says.

'But I haven't told you—'

'Oh my God, try not to be such a provincial hick when we're seen together, my plant gave me your local soon as we linked.'

I can't see her face anymore, just fingers drumming nervously on the handrail of the lift: the dim interior strobing with a faulty light source. When she speaks again her voice is at odds with the uneasy movement of her hand.

'I'm assuming by the look of that hideous can you're standing in, that you need me to take you shopping? See you shortly, darling. Prepare yourself for a spending. I won't be happy till you've joined the rest of us poor bastards in debt hell.'

The link goes dark. I smile at nothing in particular. It just feels good to be here at last; feels good to be waiting for Bel. Only … something is tainted. I don't know what; probably just the awkwardness of our long separation; my anxiety at being here; nothing. But I'm left uneasy.

'How are my two best prod-liners?'

Jakel, head of department, leans over the production bench and grins, flashing his enhanced incisors. He makes my skin itch and my insides curl away in disgust. Bel says I should learn to be more sophisticated: deviants are commonplace in the cities now. If Jakel wants to live out

101

his fantasy biting people and sucking on a bit of blood, good luck to him. There are plenty out there who enjoy getting bit.

Bel got me the job in Implant; she's in sales and I'm just an assembler so our paths rarely cross at work. I'm partnered with Amai; small, quiet, and intelligent with quick hands. She makes me look clumsy in comparison and is often rectifying my mistakes. I like her. She doesn't speak of her past and I don't ask but, from things she's let slip, I get the impression she's no stranger to the slum rings. Maybe as a consequence of her poor background or maybe from choice she's, like me, free of enhancements – excepting of course for her com-link. All firm employees are given the basic model free of charge. The pressure on me to be fitted was unrelenting and almost cost me my job. Out of desperation I feigned a reluctant confession to purity as a deviance – who knows, maybe it is – and this was accepted. My case was helped by Jakel who all too eagerly championed my cause. Unfortunately, it means I have to put up with his 'special attention'.

Jakel circles our bench and, with a hand on our shoulders, draws Amai and me together so we can both feel the pressure of his hips and groin on our backs.

'My beautiful Pures,' he breathes. 'When is one of you lovelies going to give me a little taste?'

Amai curls in on herself, hunching over the bench: it's how she deals with Jakel's advances. I'm made from different stuff. I jab my elbow into his groin and turn to confront the pointy-toothed twat. I also figure, if I draw his attention, he'll leave my friend alone.

'Go screw yourself,' I say, and give him an engaging smile.

Jakel straightens up and forces a grin. 'The more you resist, Laina, the sweeter your juice,' he says. 'Come on, just a drop.' He pulls a long pin from his lapel. 'Give me a little suck on your pinky.'

'I think the lady said to go pleasure yourself.'

Bel leans on her knuckles over the bench, her presence as always a threat and an invite: a heady mix of sexual muskiness and adrenaline. Her tail whips from side to side like a seriously pissed off cat.

'I shall,' he says. 'A great deal of pleasure – you would know if you synched with me.' He stalks away, rubbing his crotch and licking his incisors.

'God, what a pathetic little turd!' Bel plucks the manipulators from my hand. 'Come on, shift whistle about to blow, let's get out of here.'

A short, shrill sound transforms the focussed atmosphere of the prod room in an instant. Suddenly there's chatter and movement as the shift changes. I gather up my tools: the worker who takes over my station is enhanced and needs a whole different set of apparatus to do the same job. Amai has already gone; I catch a glimpse of her hurrying through to the changing pods.

'She didn't say goodbye.' I watch her slim figure till she's lost in the crowds.

'Don't think your little friend likes me,' says Bel, regarding me intensely. She smiles and resumes her normal flippant air. 'Shame, she's cute – wouldn't mind getting to know her better. P'raps we could have a threesome sometime?'

'Jesu, Bel, it was that suggestion that freaked her out!'

'Was it? Don't remember.'

Bel slips her tail round my thigh as we head for the exit.

'Oh well, can't have them all,' she says with a sigh. 'Come my pretty Pure, your turn to choose where we eat tonight.'

I wake; limbs jumbled with Bel's. The tip of her tail, inert and heavy, is coiled between my breasts and I wonder, not for the first time, how she afforded it. The dark skin of it is living tissue, seeded from her own DNA, grown through and meshed with the titanium skeleton and sensory circuitry of the plant. I run my finger along its smooth length and it shudders and tenses at my touch. The tip uncurls, questing for my nipple. There's a glint from beneath Bel's thick lashes and a slow smile spreads across her face. I knock her tail away impatiently.

'What?' she says 'you started it!' She stretches, yawning; more feline than human.

'Was just wondering how the hell you paid for this thing?' Bel's face falls; colour draining.

'Oh, Bel, what do you owe?'

Her dark eyes regard me with such sorrow that I'm unable to speak. She strokes my cheek softly, lightly and with a tenderness that tightens my heart.

'Too much …'

She kisses me with the same dark concentration as her stare and we make love with a ferocious passion I've never experienced with her before. Afterward, groggy and stupefied, there's no time for more questions as the alarm sounds.

The bed sinks into the floor leaving us sprawling and laughing as the hygiene unit swings out of the wall. My habitation space has been transformed, mostly due to Bel, although, if I'd followed all of her advice I would be in debt myself now. As it is, the bed is the only new purchase, the hygiene and cooking units were recommissioned, and the entertainment wall was a second-hand private sale. It has a few glitches but is good enough. I switch it to live feed from the exterior and the city flickers into view. The outside camera is from a high vantage point. I haven't worked out where my room is in relation to the exterior, but whenever I turn on the feed I experience a moment of disorientation, so I figure the two don't correspond. The sun hasn't broken through the heavy atmosphere, it rarely does, and the city lights strobe and glow in the smog. It looks like a fine acid drizzle has started as, down below, tiny figures hurry along beneath protective shielding that buzzes a faint blue with the moisture.

I feel closer to Bel than I ever have, more so than the days of our innocence when we would run from our families and camp on the reservations for days at a time. Something about the raw honesty of her despair and the potency of our lovemaking this morning makes me feel I have touched the real Bel for the first time. We're as stupid and fond as new lovers all the way into the heart of the city and the huge Implant building. In the echoing temple of the vast lobby we kiss with open warmth before parting for the day's work; taking separate elevators, up and down. I don't realise how precious that last soft touch and fleeting view of her face, happy and unguarded, will become.

Late to my workstation, I'm surprised to see the bench empty: Amai is not in.

'You're late for the third time this month, if it happens again I'll have to dock your credits.' Jakel brushes past. 'And now looks like your bad habits are rubbing off on your little friend. If she's not here in the next quarter personnel will have to know. Unauthorised absence can mean dismissal. If you know where she is, tell her to get her bony arse here quick.'

I slip my comm from my overalls and, keeping it out of view under the bench, try to contact Amai. There's no response: just static. I can't understand it, her implant is new and if there's a malfunction it would go to a central message. It's just dead. I keep trying for the next half hour – nothing. Jakel keeps glancing over. He looks increasingly pissed off. After nearly an hour he's back at my bench, his face creased in a frown.

'Where the hell is she,' he hisses. 'I've left it as long as I dare, I'll be in trouble as it is for not reporting her absence yet.'

'I don't know her comm-link's dead.'

'No shit?' He chews on a nail, staring at the doors as if willing her to appear. 'Can't stall any more, I'll try and fudge it, say she was feeling sick yesterday.'

'Hey, Jakel,' I call after him as he walks away. 'Thanks. You're not such an arsehole after all.'

'Does that mean I'll get a little suck for lunch?'

I give him the finger but not in the way he's expecting.

'There's gratitude!' he calls back.

As he crosses the room his face takes on the abstracted look of someone using their communication implant, but I can read the nuances of his expressions: he's not good at hiding them. Sly charm quickly dissolves and his body tenses: he's worried – no … afraid. He avoids me for the rest of the morning. Amai does not come. After lunch someone new has replaced her.

In the lobby after work Bel's deep in conversation with a suited man. She looks angry; he looks confident, condescending, sleek and well paid: a man used to power. They break off when they see me and he slips away in the crowded space. Bel puts on a bright smile.

'Darling Pretty,' she calls, 'where to tonight? No wait, it's my turn. I know just the thing – decadent as hell. Shit it makes hell look like a convent but the food's—'

'Amai's missing.'

'Who?'

'Don't – you know who – the girl I work with. She's gone, her comm's dead. Jakel won't tell me anything. I know he knows something, he's avoiding me; and she's been replaced already, some lad – he barely speaks – but I don't think he knows anything – don't think he's involved—'

'*Involved*? What are you jabbering about? You're making it sound like she's been spirited away! People leave all the time; there's no mystery. This is the city, darling!'

'She wouldn't have gone without saying something … saying goodbye …'

'Like last night?'

I don't have an answer, but it doesn't feel right. Bel has already changed the subject, is chatting happily again – about food, sex, office gossip, I don't know, I'm not listening. Her flippancy is irritating.

'Laina, are you coming?'

We're outside; the copper and glass doors thud and pop as they revolve behind us.

'No, you go ahead. I'm done in, just want an early night,' I say.

Anger darkens Bel's features: it's her go to emotion to cover pain. 'Your loss.' She stalks off; tail swishing.

The intimacy of this morning feels irretrievable. I hesitate; I don't know what to do: I'm suddenly lost. I wanted Bel to go away but beyond that I hadn't thought any further. I don't want to go home. I stare at the seething crowds. As usual the city is a mass of movement, so it's the stillness that attracts my attention: a small figure across the street is watching the building intently – a girl – there's something familiar about her.

Crossing directly is impossible: the automated traffic is too fast and too dense. I'll have to take the underpass. The girl is still immobile; focussed on the doors behind me. I consider attracting her attention, get her to wait, but don't want to spook her. The subway is close but the crush of commuters is at a virtual standstill; squashed into the bottle neck of an entrance. I shove and trample through, ignoring the protests and insults. I hate these tunnels at the best of times and avoid them if I can. My chest tightens and black spots swim in front of my eyes: the press of humanity is claustrophobic. I emerge sweating and gasping for air, and have to wait for my vision to clear. The girl is gone.

Shit.

She had been standing at the top of a flight of steps that once gave access to the road. Wire fencing has been put up to try and dissuade anyone stupid enough to contemplate crossing the traffic. It was the perfect vantage point to observe the entrance to Implant. I'm staring across the street, unsure what to do, how to find her, when the hairs on the back of my neck prickle. Someone's watching me. I turn and scan the crowd, most people have their heads down, no one is looking my way. There are no windows at street level and the ones higher up are one way mirror glass; impossible to tell if I'm being observed from anywhere in there. Along the street is a break between the buildings: a narrow service alley. A slight movement catches my eye. Ah …

The passage is dark; barely the width of two people. Ducts and pipes pepper the walls making it seem an even tighter space. Both buildings are at least twenty stories and the light is fading anyway so further in, away from the illumination of the street, it looks pitch-black. I feel my way in the gloom. The place is thick with refuse. I slip on something slimy and swear under my breath. Something scurries over my foot and I bite back a scream. The sound of the street gradually fades behind the hum of vents and maintenance machinery. In the dim light I can see a set of metal doors in one of the walls and in the recess a shadowy figure.

'Hello,' I say, 'I won't hurt you.'

The girl steps out but keeps her distance: alert and guarded. She looks about twelve, small and thin, and is dressed in worn faded clothes. The jacket is too large: maybe a hand-me-down she hasn't grown into yet, maybe all she can get. She's clean though and someone has made an effort to mend and patch her coveralls – so, poor, but not destitute.

'Are you Laina?' She says shifting nervously. Everything about her is tense: ready to run. Then it dawns on me why she's so familiar.

'You're Amai's …?'

'Sister.'

'Of course, she never really speaks about home, but I'm sure she mentioned you—'

'You're Laina?'

'Yes.'

'She speaks of *you* often. Where is she? What's happened? Please …'

The girl's voice falters and I can see she's fighting back tears. My stomach knots. 'I don't know; I've been trying her comm all day.'

'It's dead: been that way since last night,' the girl says. 'I spoke to her when she finished shift; said she'd been called into Fitting to have the three month service. When she wasn't home by ten I tried the link and just got static. I begged her not to get the link but she said she'd lose her job without it.'

'What's wrong with having a link?'

The girl hesitates, and gives me an appraising look. She clearly doesn't trust me.

'Have heard rumours, that's all … it's nothing. They won't let me into the building; can you ask in Fitting if they saw her?'

'Sure, I'll go now. Can you wait here?'

'Not safe, curfew nearly down and I have to be back in the outer ring. Will you come there?'

'Yes.'

'I'll wait at checkpoint nine. Be careful Laina.'

She slips out of the alley, melting into the crowd. I'm left uneasy; my stomach churns, and I realise I never asked her name.

It takes some persuading to get back into Implant: workers don't usually want to return after shift. I convince security that I've finally plucked up the courage to talk to Fitting about a comm-link and if I don't do it now I never will. I'm known throughout the company as Liana the Pure, so my change of heart is a matter of immense delight. The guards enjoy taking the piss before they let me pass.

Fitting is in sub-basement three. The manufacturing floors are twenty-four seven but everywhere else is office hours only, so it's strangely quiet when the lift doors open. Security checked so I know there will be someone in the department, but the corridor is empty and silent except for the soft hum of generators. Frosted glass doors at the far end show bright lights beyond. My mouth is dry and my palms sweaty. This is stupid: I've let the girl spook me. I just need to ask if they saw Amai and if she mentioned where she was going afterwards. No big deal. I step out of the lift and a man suddenly emerges from a side door dragging a cart laden with cleaning stuff.

'Oh,' I try and get my heart to stop racing. 'Didn't know the company had cleaners?'

'Automation system's bust. Got me in last week. S'pect they'll boot me out soon as it's fixed. Sorry if I gave you a fright.'

I mumble 'ok,' and sidle past. As I'm half way down the corridor he speaks again.

'Gave the other one a fright last night ... seems folk ain't used to seein' people do honest work no more.'

'Other one? '

'Yesterday, 'bout this time. Young like you but not so pretty.' The man leers at me but when I don't respond he continues. 'Sweet girl; took the time to chat. Said she was here for a service. I said—'

I hold up my old comm-link to show him a picture of Amai.

'Aye, that's the lass. Nice girl.'

Thanking him, I head for the glass doors. So she was definitely here. I feel less jumpy; maybe she said something in Fitting about where she was headed next. As I reach out for the palm panel to open the door, the man speaks again.

'Watch yourself in there,' he says, and trundles into another office along the corridor.

The frosted doors of Fitting slide open.

A Tech is sitting at a broad desk reading through some papers. He looks up and for a fleeting moment a look of surprise, almost panic, flits across his face. 'The department's closed,' he says and shuffles the jumble of papers into a file.

Something about his manner and the warnings I've had make me cautious. I decide to stick to the story I've given security. So, with a broad smile I introduce myself and stride forward as if to shake his hand, hoping to get a look at the name on the file. It's slid into a drawer before I can get near enough. He doesn't return my smile or take my proffered hand.

'We're closed, contact the department Monday and make an appointment.'

I stumble through the story, but he doesn't look like he's buying it. I'm starting to sweat. Oh, well, here goes nothing ...

'I've been dead set against have an implant till my friend had one a few months ago. She's been raving about how brilliant it is; so, I'm persuaded. You probably remember her; she was down here last night for her three month service ... Amai – Amai Torvald?'

'The department was closed last night and we don't do a service unless something malfunctions.'

'Oh! I'm sure she came. It was after shift – about seven?'

'You're mistaken, the department was closed at five yesterday, same as every day. No one was here.'

My stomach tightens and the hairs prickle on my neck. I need to get out. Gabbling an apology and promises to call after the weekend, I retreat back through the doors, thanking him for his time. The Tech remains immobile and silent, watching me leave. Just before the doors hiss shut, I hear him speak; I don't know if it's a comm-link or whether someone else is in the room: someone I hadn't noticed. 'We may have a problem,' he says.

The doors click locked. The thick glass prevents me from hearing any more. As I hurry to the lifts, I keep checking over my shoulder, not looking where I'm going, and crash into the cleaner.

'Steady!'

'Sorry!'

'That was quick! You're out sooner than the other lassie.'

'You saw her leave then?' Relief floods through me – this has been a misunderstanding after all – I've let my imagination run riot – what a tit! Bel's going to piss herself laughing when I tell her.

'No, that's not what I'm sayin': she didn't come out. Not while I was here anyways.'

My heart misses a beat. I jab at the lift call; I've got to get out: the walls are closing in. The cleaner must have noticed my face fall as his tone's apologetic.

'I was here till just gone ten … no one came out but the light was still on down there … maybe she—'

I don't wait to hear anymore; the lift opens and I stumble inside. Along the corridor the frosted doors click, hissing open. Frantic, I thump the lift buttons keeping my eyes on the bright space beyond the glass. No one emerges but I can't breathe till the lift closes and I'm ascending to the lobby. God, what am I getting myself into?

I've never been into the outer rings – the industrial districts; the slums. I know checkpoint nine though: most of the clubs Bel has taken me to are close to the checkpoints; places on the edge in every sense. I wish she was with me: I'm afraid. Her lust for life always dispels the darkness, always has. I've tried linking but it went straight to message: she must still be mad. I haven't tried again, I'm worried about the stuff Amai's sister said; worried they'll trace me through the comm, listen in on the conversation. Who "they" are I don't know – if they're anyone! I'm getting paranoid. Get a grip!

Even though it's late I don't have any trouble at the checkpoint: questions are rarely asked. Inhabitants of the inner ring often seek distraction, adventure, a bit of rough, drugs, maybe even try and do some good in the slums. The guard scans my identity tattoo and waves me through with barely a glance: holo-sport is playing in the cabin and he hurries back as his colleague whoops at a score.

113

The most noticeable difference beyond the checkpoint is the dark. The inner ring is ablaze day and night; a glittering jewel of commerce and consumption; here energy is precious; limited. Light-headed, legs shaking, afraid and alone, I walk into the night-black streets. The girl isn't here. What if she doesn't come? The streets are narrow, convoluted, filled with filth. My head spins. Figures bump me in the gloom. Shadowy figures I can't see, the world spins, I graze my cheek on a wall, darkness, spinning, 'catch her', no … I lash out and fall.

'Laina … Laina, it's ok, you're ok.'
I stop struggling and blink to adjust my eyes to the light: it seems very bright. Then a face comes into focus: Aima's sister. I relax.
'You passed out – sorry I wasn't at the gate – lucky I found you. We're at a friend's house.'
A man's profile swims into view, he turns and smiles, passes me a glass of water. I sit up gingerly and take a sip, the world is still tilting.
'When did you last eat?' he asks.
'This morning.'
He grunts and leaves the room. I tell the girl about Fitting and before I finish he's back with a cup of broth.
'It's a bad idea to go poking around there, those people are dangerous,' he says. 'Hanah, why did you let her do this?'
So, her name's Hanah. I swallow some of the broth and immediately feel a little better.
'I shouldn't have asked you to go, I'm sorry,' she says.
'What are you talking about? How are they dangerous? It's ridiculous!' I laugh, now I'm safe, the whole episode seems foolish.
'There are rumours,' the man says, he isn't smiling. 'People go missing.'

'Oh, come on …'

'You know that to fit an implant they have to make space,' he taps his head, 'in here.'

'Of course, it's perfectly safe.' I say, but it's one of the reasons I'm reluctant to have the procedure.

'Safe?'

'There are risks, sure …'

'It goes wrong more than you'd believe – more than they'll let on – more than it should.'

'Where are all the casualties then? What's done with them? We would know.'

'They're careful who they choose. Those without connections or family, people who won't be missed, the ones no one cares about, the poor.'

'Well that proves your theory is bullshit – Amai has family.'

'Did she ever speak of me at work?' says Hanah. 'Does the company even know about me?'

'… well …'

'I told her it was stupid! That she wasn't protecting me, just putting herself at risk. Oh, Amai, why didn't you listen?'

Hanah bolts from the room. I stare at the man in shock.

'What do you think's happened to Amai?'

'Sold.'

I laugh. 'What to the body snatchers?'

'She wasn't dead – not technically. The slave trade is booming.'

I'm not laughing now. My skin prickles and I can taste the broth in my throat.

'People go in willingly to have the plant and when the bastards are in here,' he taps his head again, 'making space; the person gets erased; memories, personality, everything that makes them who they are. And the living husk is sold – as a sex slave, a chem-worker, a punch bag, a wife – whatever you've ordered those boys in Fitting will find you a match.'

'Absurd! You're insane!' I can't believe I'm listening to this crap.

'You need to be careful, lady, I hear there's collectors out there pay big money for a Pure like you.'

Hanah is back in the doorway leaning heavily on the frame; her face ashen.

'This is shit, Hanah. I'll find Amai, I promise.'

Back out on the street I hear the man call from inside: '*Big* money!'

Once I'm through the checkpoint, I risk linking Bel again. I really need to see her; be enveloped in her warmth; enjoy her take on the absurdity of tonight. She answers.

'Hey.'

'Hey, yerself.'

There's no vis and I hear a man's voice: 'that her?' I know Bel isn't exclusive to me: I don't see her for days, sometimes weeks at a time, but to hear the evidence unsettles me.

'Sorry, you're busy,' I mumble.

'It was you blew *me* out remember? What's up, you sound weird?'

'Yeah, it's been a weird night!'

'Tell your Aunty Bel all about it then.'

'Not over the comms; I've heard some stuff and … well I'm not sure linking is safe. Can we talk face to face?'

'Darling if you want to see me you just have to say, not go all cloak and dagger. Rene's will just be getting lively by now, meet me there, half an hour.'

The link goes dead. I breathe easily, a weight lifted. Bel is going to find my adventure hilarious and you can bet she won't let me forget how gullible I've been for a long time to come.

Rene's Bar is a dive in the twisted alleys behind Implant. Bel was right, even though it's gone midnight the place is only just getting going. I squeeze into the sweaty crowd; wondering how I'll find her in the press of bodies. The place pulses with the buzz of hedonistic pleasure jacked into the rising tempo of the music. A warm pressure coils round my waist: Bel's tail. She draws me through the mass of throbbing bodies to the booths at the back of the room.

'Hey, Douggie, how you been?' Bel addresses a rangy man with tiger stripes and very green eyes who's lounging in one of the booths. 'How 'bout you scram so I can have a clandestine chat with my little friend here? I'll owe you.'

'The usual?'

'Don't you ever get tired of it?'

'Not with you.'

'How 'bout I throw in ...' she leans forward and whispers in his ear. His eyes go wide and he grins.

'I'll get Rene to send over drinks for that!' He gives me a wink as he slides out to let us in.

High padded seats muffle the sounds of the bar. I suddenly feel tense; unsure of what to say, how to begin. Bel chats about the clientele, who's doing who; who wants to do who; until our drinks arrive and I launch into the evening's events. By the time I've finished she's laughing so hard, tears are streaming down her face.

'Oh my poor baby!' She crushes me in a hug. 'What a time you've had.' Throwing back her head, she roars again. 'Wish I'd been there! Oh, I know! Let's break into Fitting and get a look at that mysterious folder?'

'Yeah, ha ha, laugh it up.'

'I'm deadly serious.'

Bel isn't laughing anymore; she's staring at me intently.

'It would be madness!'

'The perfect end to your crazy adventure … come on let's do it!'

'And impossible—'

'Maybe not: I know the codes for the back entrance, and we're not going to steal anything so it's not really breaking and entering … say yes.'

'It's insane…' but I've promised to find Amai and whatever's in that file may be my only lead. What the hell; don't have a better plan.

The basement levels are deserted; the silence eerie; just the low hum of the generators. I can't stop giggling: this is so ludicrous. We make it to the corridor outside Fitting without being challenged. It's in darkness.

'Your turn,' says Bel, 'are you still any good at picking locks?'

'There's much to recommend a misspent youth.' I smile at her and have to control another wave of hysteria before getting started on the door panel.

It takes me a while: locks have changed since I was a kid. Eventually there's a satisfying click and with a hiss the door slides open. 'Ta da…'

Bel pulls me into a tight embrace and a passionate kiss. After a while I pull away. 'Not exactly the time and place!'

'Always the time and place for you,' she says smiling, but her voice is heavy with sadness.

I don't have time for one of her mood swings as I'm worried I've triggered an alarm. Hurrying round the desk I try the drawer; it isn't locked. The top file has Amai's name on it.

'Found it.' I grin but Bel's frowning at something behind me. A sharp sting burns the back of my neck and I can't move. *Paralysed.*

Bel turns away. *What?* The tech from earlier walks out from behind me and joins her in the doorway. I struggle to shout, get Bel's attention, but I can't speak. *This isn't happening!*

'Bit late for a call,' he says, 'in future I'd rather arrange delivery with more notice.'

'Had to be now, you know why.' Bel's voice is flat, emotionless.

Please turn round? The joke's gone far enough! Please turn round!

'Are we all square?' says Bel, she still won't look at me.

'For this one?' The tech glances over. 'Sure, you're all paid up. Till you want the next implant.' He laughs.

I can see Bel's profile, her jaw is clenched. *Bel, you're frightening me.* She walks away.

Oh God, Bel, please come back. You bloody selfish bitch, please…

Another tech comes and they lift me into the back room. *Bel.* I can't move or speak; I can breathe – barely – and blink and that's it. *Bel, don't leave me!*

'Are we fitting this one with anything?' It's the tech I haven't seen before.

'No, this one's for The Collector. He said any Pures are for him, any price but they have to be unadulterated. This one's perfect, he'll pay a fortune.'

'We not erasing her then?'

'Course we are! Everything has to go, he's very particular; memories, personality; the lot – she has to be wiped clean.'

This can't be happening! Bel, you bitch, walk back in, help me for fu—

They're strapping something round my head, attaching electrodes to my temples. *Please, God don't!*

'What's he do with them?'

'He's started some kind of breeding programme.'

'Yeah, right! Dirty bugger.' They both laugh.

Laugh! She'll kick your arse for that…Bel…

'He's trying to keep the pure line untainted. Thinks he's saving humanity. Councillor Fraike: saviour of the human race!'

My uncle! This is a mistake, he's my uncle. For God's sake you've made a mistake. You have to stop, it's a mistake!

'Put something between her teeth: don't want her biting half her tongue off.'

Get off you bastards this is a mistake! Bel—

Something clicks; there's buzzing in my head.

Bel, BelpleasepleaseGodhelp me…

Please… …help… … …m—

Celebrity

I've become a bit of a celebrity. It was all down to Mrs Pargiter's granddaughter's school project. She had to do something or other about technology, I couldn't quite grasp what the thing was about, but the up-shot was that she wanted to video our annual general meeting of the Stroud branch of the WI. I'm the general secretary and I did a speech on Macramé. It's a dying art, so you can imagine my delight when the video went viral. My daughter explained what that means. What it boils down to is that I am now quite famous and our branch of the WI is known right across the county, maybe even the whole of Britain, possibly the world if you believe what they say about the world web.

I haven't seen the video yet, my daughter keeps making excuses to not show it to me – she says her computer is down. Down where? She's always looking at things on her Smarts phone so I don't see why she can't show it to me on that. It's a bit strange and, to be honest, somewhat vexing. So I'm off into town to our one remaining library – don't get me started about that – so my friend Margery who volunteers there on a Tuesday can log me up to a computer.

By the time I get to the bus stop the sunny morning is fading into a dull afternoon. I check my handbag for my pack-away plastic rain poncho. It's always best to be prepared. That's something my great Aunt Sadie taught me along with never be seen in public without lipstick on and don't stint when pouring Gin. A couple of the neighbourhood teenage girls are already at the stop. One of them obviously recognises me and whispers behind her hand to her friend. They gawp at me goggle-eyed, giggling and making odd and slightly rude blurting noises – strange how celebrity can affect the masses. 'Are you practitioners of the Hitch knot?' I ask, and the pair of them dissolve beneath a wave of hilarity. No manners the youth of today and they don't seem to have any social skills. In my day if an elder of the community and one that's obviously out of your social league as I surely am now I'm part of the Glitterati, engaged you in social chit-chat you would respond with some civility. I leave them clinging to each other in helpless spasms of mirth as I board the bus.

The number nine is busy for a Tuesday and I'm forced to take a seat next to a rather desiccated creature at the back. It turns out to be Mrs Withers. I thought the poor old thing was dead but she must have just been very ill from the look of her. She stares out at the girls who are still laughing and pointing. I give them a wave before the bus lurches off that seems to delight them still further. Mrs Withers turns her baleful stare to me. I suppose an explanation is required.

'I expect you're wondering what that was all about?'

Mrs Withers just keeps staring.

I plough on doggedly: 'A speech I gave has got onto U tube and has gone viral.'

'Oh, you poor dear,' she says suddenly animated. 'There's nothing they can do about that is there? Now if it was an infection they could give you antibiotics, you'll just have to ride it out, that's what my doctor says to me all the time, I think it's just an excuse for him to do nothing, they don't want to know these days, and you can never get to see them, I have to know I'm going to be ill two weeks in advance if I want an appointment so I tend to book a couple every month just in case, ah, here comes my stop.' She dings the dinger several times more than is necessary. 'You look after yourself and keep those tubes wrapped up; I'm a great believer in honey and lemon taken in a tumbler of hot whiskey.'

I bet she is.

She staggers down the bus grabbing at the poles as we speed along, her enormous handbag smacking into the backs of heads as she progresses. I hold my breath as she advances on Colonel Bolkinghorne from over Woodchester way, who's sitting at the front. I've always been dubious of his full head of red hair: he must be nintey if he's a day. The terrible bag thwacks him on the back of the head, and yes, there is definite slippage.

The bus screeches to a halt at Mrs Withers' stop, spinning her into the luggage rack. There's a bit of a delay after that as the colonel and a lady who works at one of the charity shops in town, untangle her from a large tartan shopper and get her back on her feet. The colonel, now with his toupee at a jaunty angle over one ear, helps her off the bus. Then there's a further delay when it turns out the tartan shopper belongs to Mrs Withers. The colonel retrieves it and is presumably being thanked by Mrs Withers as she won't let go of his hand and is talking nineteen to the dozen about something, when the bus doors slide shut and the driver puts her foot down: she probably has quite a bit of time to make up now. The colonel starts waving frantically and shouting as Mrs Withers tootles off up the road.

I'm feeling a bit miffed that Mrs Withers got the wrong end of the stick like that, and she didn't give me the chance to explain. I have my suspicions that she knew all along what I was on about as their branch of the WI had lessons on sailing the web last summer. She's been in the local paper with her prize winning crochet and is the sort that would begrudge someone else a bit of notoriety. I turn to give the colonel a wave. The poor man is now red in the face and shouting something. I hastily turn away, my own face turning the same colour as his: I used to work in a factory as a girl and learnt to lip read, and here was me thinking all these years that he was a gentleman.

The computers are in the reference section of the library. It's pretty busy and a whisper starts as Margery and I enter the room: people have recognised me of course. I smile regally and try to look aloof. There's a lot of nudging and peering over screens and round bookcases as we head for an empty booth. Margery gets more and more flustered as she sets me up for the viewing.
'Are you sure you want to do this here … in such a public place?' she whispers going extremely red.
She always was a wilting flower when it came to public speaking and so forth.
'What if you don't like what you see …' she says, wringing her hands, the epitome of embarrassed spinsterhood. 'It can sometimes come as a shock to see yourself on film.'
'Don't be silly, Margery, I'm quite used to being filmed,' I counter robustly, 'my daughter is always at it with her phone.'
'Yes, but what if …'
'PLAY IT, MARGERY.'
She hits a key with a small whimper and scuttles out of the room. There is complete silence in here now and an air of tense expectation, which is very gratifying: I assume everyone is quite excited for the chance to hear my Macramé talk again with me present. There will no doubt

be questions afterwards, and maybe I'll be able to give a small demonstration. I always carry a bit of wool in my bag for those little darning emergencies.

The film begins. I seem to be quite a long way away and my voice is not as clear as I would have wished. I remember now, Mrs Pargiter's granddaughter had to set up in the aisle at the rear of the hall to avoid blocking the view for any of the ladies in attendance. She was next to Eugenia Dowrick, who always sits in the back row due to the necessity of being near the facilities. She's a martyr to her affliction. The first creation I hold up is my little man – my own design, but one of my simpler pieces of knotting that even a beginner can attempt. At this point an unfortunate noise drowns out my narrative. Eugenia's troubles are not always silent ones and are the reason we have to travel with all the windows open when we go anywhere on the minibus.

Behind a bookcase in the reference room, I can hear someone trying to repress a giggle. Back on the screen I'm holding up several of my small knotted figures and, to do so easily, I often slot a finger through the wool-work of one or other of them. I realise now that I could have been more mindful of where on my little man my finger poked through. The film starts to wobble a bit for some reason – I don't think Mrs Pargiter's granddaughter will get very high marks if she can't even hold the camera still. I notice the person at the computer next to me has stuffed their scarf in their mouth and has gone quite scarlet. The film has jumped to the next object. I'm holding up one of my 3D creations of which I am justifiably proud: this is advanced, ground-breaking craft work, using a new technique of my own devising. The piece is a pug dog. Just as I'm lifting the tail the better to show the intricate plaiting, Eugenia's affliction makes itself heard in a loud and protracted way. The film ends right there. Not a glimpse of my demonstration of speed-knotting or a fraction even of the lively debate had by all afterwards on string versus wool.

There are parps and squeaks around the room as everyone tries to hold in their laughter.

I see.

That's how it is.

It would seem I am not the new champion of crafting as I had so fondly believed. No, indeed, that is not to be my lot. Now I understand what my daughter was trying to protect me from and why Margery showed such hesitation. Well, life doesn't always deal you the hand you want. Aunt Sadie used to tell me that. She lived fast and died young; she was barely into her seventies when the side-car she was travelling in became unhitched from her boyfriend's Norton and she flew, for a short while at least, from Beachy Head. 'A girl like you has to learn to make the best of things, Joan,' she would say, 'if you aren't dealt a winning hand – bluff.' These are definitely not the cards I was expecting, but Aunt Sadie's blood runs strong in my veins.

I stand, drawing myself up to my full height. Dignity, that's how to face this situation. The eyes of the room are on me.

After a long intake of breath I let rip with 'thffffththththththththffffffppppppppt' the loudest and longest raspberry I can muster before making a gesture with my middle finger.

The room erupts.

Suddenly I'm surrounded by a crowd of youngsters, whooping and patting me on the back and getting me to do high claps with them and teaching me to fist bump. Apparently I'm a ledge. Margery hurries in looking worried just as I start signing things for people and rather rudely snatches away the reference book on pond life I'm about to autograph. My head's in a whirl as she ushers me out and into romantic fiction: I've never been a popular icon for the youth of the day before.

'I'm so sorry you had to find out about the film,' Margery says, totally and wilfully to my mind, misreading the situation. 'Do you want to slip out the staff exit at the back? You can cut through Poundland and catch the number nine home without too much fuss.'

'Don't be ridiculous, Margery, my public awaits.'

She gives me a look I can't begin to read and, inexplicably, there are tears in her eyes.

The glass doors at the front entrance are steamed up. Outside it's pouring down. While I'm rummaging in my handbag for my plastic rain poncho, I find my clip on shades. I click them into place, check my lipstick, adjust my plastic hood, and step out into the rain.

Lightning Source UK Ltd.
Milton Keynes UK
UKHW051416091220
374827UK00033B/1461

9 781838 203405